TWO SWORDS

Tim Crets

Contents

Prologue

Asman ran as the screams of his village rang through the air.

The day had been peaceful and calm, but as night came over the small town, it was overwhelmed by what was shockingly their own military.

Felias was one of the largest kingdoms to the south, and Asmans village was apart of that kingdom; so why was their own army slaughtering the citizens of Thamor?

Asman had been with his brother when the soldiers invaded. They were just beginning to turn in for the night as the first of the screams started.

His brother, Samdel, told him to run, but it took Asman seeing his brothers throat slit by a soldier for him to finally do so.

Asman had no time for tears as he focused on weaving away from either another dying friend clutching for his ankle, or a sword wielding guard member that was aiming to kill him.

He ran past all the houses that were lit aflame, no doubt in an effort to smoke all the people hiding in them out and into the blade awaiting them.

As he turned his head to look to his right, there was abruptly a sharp pain to his left shoulder. Asman hit the ground harshly on his hands and knees, the gravel from the road biting into his palms.

When he whipped his head back to look at what it was, he saw another soldier standing over him with a sword bloodied by likely Asman's blood.

The guards face was blank as he rose his blade again, focused at Asman's sweat and dirt caked throat.

Asman inhaled sharply and dodged the sword just as it came down, his and the guards face morphed into one of shock.

When the soldier gritted his teeth and lifted the sword once more, Asman took the chance to scramble to his feet and bolt back between the houses.

He had been raised in this village, so he knew that between Lady Camania and Glaverd the tailors houses, there was a gate to where the Lady had a small garden that branched off into the forest. Asman felt that the soldier was still following him just before Asman shot to the narrow space between the stucco coated homes, but seeing as the soldier was much bigger, Asman was able to slip through quickly and lose the man.

The gate to the garden slammed open as Asman flung himself into it, uncaring of the tiny wooden stick keeping it closed against the wind.

Asman did not glance back while he continued to sprint out and away from the village, barely dodging the trees in the dim light from his burning home.

His lungs ached from both the running and the smoke that he had inhaled while squeezing between the houses.

It was not until the village was no where to be seen that he finally stopped and fell to his knees.

He was alone, and lost. His brother was dead and his home gone.

Was there a point to running, or did he just walk into a slow and starved death instead of a quick and bloody one?

Chapter One: Fire

The blood from Asman's wound was beginning to worry him.

The night was cold, and dark, and full of sounds that previously would not have scared him, but now shook him to the core at the thought of a pack of wolves smelling his shoulder and coming to finish him off.

Asman had denied himself the ability to cry, as he did not know when he would come to water again, and it was best to conserve his fluids.

Though, at the rate that he was bleeding, he was sure that he would not make it through the night.

The tunic he had put on for night was long sleeved, but did little to curb the chill of night. His trousers were ripped at the knees and his feet torn to shreds from the ground.

There had been no need for shoes when he was about to tuck into his bed.

Him and his brother had finished their work for the day and already had eaten dinner before it all happened. They both ran the village butchery, seeing as it was their fathers job before he passed away from illness.

Their mother had passed after Asman's birth, though Samdel said he had barely knew her since he was only a few summers older than Asman.

Samdel was almost thirty winters. He was just as young as Asman; he should have died at sixty, or at least fighting in a battle. Samdel was brave, and he did not deserve to die in the same way they killed the chickens for meat.

Asman exhaled shakily and focused on the ground in front of him, though there was little use as the night was pitch black and the only light was coming from the waning moon above.

Even if he had been in these woods before, he doubted he would be able to tell where he was. Each step sent a shiver of pain through his body, his mind clouded with the feeling of his back soaked with blood.

The sticks and stones digging into his feet hardly even felt like anything. The cold chilled wind was nothing, he had stopped shivering perhaps an hour ago.

His eyes kept shutting on their own, but he kept walking and hardly avoiding trees.

As his eyes slipped closed once again, his left shoulder connected with a tree, sending a blinding pain all throughout his body that sent him to the ground.

Asman barely gasped before his eyes rolled back into his head and he fell unconscious.

———————————

There was a warmness when he awoke.

His shoulder was still throbbing, but he could not feel any fresh blood.

He was also on his stomach, and on a fur, with the scent of a fire and food lacing the air.

Asman's eyes widened and he attempted to lift himself up, but slammed back to the ground as his wound made his arm give out.

It was light out and the sun on his back was what probably made him so warm.

There were people talking, yet not loud enough for him to catch what was being said. Nobody was in front or to the side of him so he could not see anything but the open expanse of forest.

After a few deep breaths, he controlled the pain and managed to use his right arm to lift himself up so that he was facing the voices. He could feel stitches pulling at the side of the wound.

Asman's breath stuttered as he saw who was there.

Likely around twenty people, all of them staring at him with curious looks. Some of them were men, and some women, most of them were holding a bowl or plate full of stew.

Asman froze as they stared and he stared back, his eyes glancing around nervously until they landed on the one tent in the clearing fluttering open.

The man that stepped out was similar to those sitting around the few small fires; rugged and muscular, with scrutinizing eyes that had Asman's heart beating quick with anxiety.

After a few moments, the man spoke lowly to one of the women sitting nearby and disappeared back into the tent. The woman nodded and shoved a spoonful of stew into her mouth before standing.

Asman flinched as she approached him, her face not showing any anger, but not any kindness either.

"Come. Up with you." She said and bent down to lightly take Asman's right arm in her grip.

Asman hissed softly but did not resist the help in standing. Instead, he let himself be pulled from the fur laid on the ground and towards the tent where the man was.

The other habitants of the camp glanced once more before they returned to talking and occasionally laughing; as if Asman was not a stranger being hauled into a tent with what was probably their leader.

The woman with her hand still on his arm did not seem malicious in her movements and went slow even if the tent was across the clearing.

Once they reached the tent, the woman opened the flaps and guided Asman in, letting go of his arm as soon as the flaps closed behind them. He was confused as to all that was happening.

The man from before was seated at a small travel desk, with only a small stool under him as a seat. As he saw Asman and the woman enter, he sighed and waved a hand to dismiss her.

She nodded once more and then turned to Asman, smiled, and then thwacked him on his right shoulder before leaving the tent.

Asman exhaled sharply as, even if it was not his right shoulder that was injured, the movement rattled his body and sent lightning bolts of pain throughout his left side.

The man did not say anything about the woman's actions, and instead stood from his stool and walked over to Asman. The latter watched him with keen eyes while the man stopped in front him and stared down into Asman's eyes.

The man was only slightly taller than him, but with how muscled the man was, it felt like Asman was enveloped beneath the man.

"Where are you from?"

Asman furrowed his brows slightly and ignored the pang in his chest, he only stared back up into the mans grey-blue eyes as if he looked away something bad would happen.

"Nowhere. Not anymore." Asman responded while trying to mask his sadness. His voice shook from misuse and fear.

The mans eyebrows only slightly twitched together, but his face was soon blank again.

"How did you get your wound?"

"A sword."

Asman did not feel that the man was asking for any bad reasons, but Asman also felt as if he needed to be careful with a man that he had never met before.

He had woken up somewhere in the forest, with his wound stitched and a large group of people surrounding him; the situation was far too confusing for him to reveal any personal details about his life.

"Was there a reason that a sword found its way into your shoulder?" The man crossed his arms and Asman felt his heart thud with fear.

"... I suppose so. But, I do not know the reason personally." Asman shrugged slightly and finally broke eye contact with the man.

The man nodded and continued to look down at Asman, his face inquiring even if he knew what Asman was doing.

"What is your name?" The man asked finally after what seemed like some deliberation.

Asman paused and stared off at the ground. Would there be a reason not to tell the man his name? It was not as if anyone who ever knew him was alive still; there was no need to protect anyone. He was alone.

"Asman." He said with what was probably a noticeable sadness.

He would have preferred to be asking the man questions. Like, where was he? Who was this man and this group? Why had they helped him?

"Where are you from, Asman?" The man asked.

Asman furrowed his brows and looked back up at the man.

"I already told you, it does not matter anymore." Asman clicked his tongue in annoyance. "Why am I here? Why not leave me in the forest to die?"

Perhaps Asman's words were too harsh, because in the next second, he was being held up by his throat against one of the poles keeping the tent up.

"Are you from Felias or Isadren?" The man growled, his once plain face now cold and demanding.

Asman struggled against the grip weakly and grasped at the mans hands as they barely squeezed his throat, but cut off the circulation to and from his head.

"Neither." Asman growled back, he knew who these people were now.

They were Isadrenians; a large rival to Felias and the largest kingdom from the north. Asman assumes that they were some sort of scouting party or small militia with how close to the Felias Capital they actually were.

"I am not affiliated with either kingdoms anymore. My village was Feliasian but the army fucking burned it down, so I no longer give two shits about any side of a stupid and ignorant war." Asman hissed out, this time not breaking eye contact as his toes barely skimmed the ground.

The pole was digging into his back, but very clearly was favoring his right side. He was beginning to think this man was deliberately holding him in a way so that he was not actually hurt.

The man also seemed to become confused at Asman's words and loosened his grip, enough so that Asman's feet hit the ground once more and the mans hand was only sitting around his neck but not squeezing.

"Your own army attacked your village?" The man asked as his face no longer showed any angry.

"Yes, and I would like to know why you kept me alive when everyone I have ever known is likely dead by now." Asman was not the same as the man, and was becoming more and more irritable.

He was in pain, in a foreign place, withholding the tears he wanted to shed for his brother, and now a strange man was holding his neck as if they were lovers.

The man had dark auburn hair that was pulled back with a leather tie, and Asman could see once he was close enough that the mans dusting of a beard was the same color.

Asman would not deny the man was attractive, but was also irritating Asman more than someone who had previously held his neck like that would have.

"You would have rather me left you to die?" The man still seemed confused. "We found you barely breathing in the middle of the forest last night, and you believe that I would leave you there? I do not know what Feliasians do in that situation, but in Isadren we do not do such cruel things."

Asman only kept the mans gaze, his breathing quicker than normal and both his hands wrapped around the mans wrists.

The man stared back, and soon enough, he let go of Asman's neck and backed away.

"You are coming with us back to Isadren." The man suddenly said, causing Asman to scoff and begin to say something before the man interrupted. "I do not care what you think on the matter; the Queen will need to hear about Felias launching attacks within its own country. You will be proof of the attack as the only survivor."

"So then I am a prisoner? You speak of not leaving me to die and instead think to keep me captive, taking me north all so that I can recount what was one of the horrific days of my life?" Asman frowned and gently rolled his shoulders to stretch his muscles, hiss once more when his shoulder burned. "I would have rather died than allow you to take me to fucking Isadren."

The man turned around once more to face Asman, the latter did not like the look on his face.

"Oh, so you are like all the other Feliasians? Taught to believe you are the best kingdom on the continent?" The man squinted at Asman. "There is a war happening, and whether you think it is ignorant or not, the actions made now will determine how life is lived for the rest of us. I would rather not be in your situation and see everyone I care for slaughtered."

Asman exhaled lowly, the sound slightly turning into a growl as he rolled his eyes.

"I did not mean it like that. I told you I no longer see myself as Feliasian, and even though I do not trust you, trust me when I tell you that I never truly felt like one previously either."

"How do I even know that you are telling the truth about your village? This could be a scheme by Felias' king to breach the Isadrenians ranks." The man inquired with a sudden wariness.

Asman huffed and went to cross his arms, but paused when the stitches pulled uncomfortably.

"If it were my choice, I would be dead; does that not tell a certainty of my ambitions staying within your... scouting group, or whatever this is?" Asman waved a dismissive hand to the space behind him, where the flaps to the tent were still shut tight.

"We are called the Blood Guards. We are the personal soldiers of the Queen, and send back all the information she needs to keep Isadren safe." The man said and sat himself down at the desk again. Asman nearly snorted at the name. "We were already on our way home when you were found. It is only two fortnights ride from here to Isadren and we will stop by Stelai to restock our supplies."

The man looked to the stack of papers on the desk and picked one up before doing so with a pen also, the sound of scratching filling the air as he began to write.

"I suggest you get rest tonight. Unfortunately, Stelai is still a day away, and we did not plan for another to join us, so you will have to walk while we ride. Dahlia will feed you. Goodnight, Asman."

Asman wished he could have thought of something to say, but the man had enough dominance in his last few words that Asman felt it was more of an order.

He silently left the tent and ignored the looks that the 'Blood Guards' were giving him.

The woman from before was the first to say something after she approached him.

"Here; some stew we saved for you." She said with a smile and handed a bowl of said stew over to Asman.

Asman nodded in thanks and took the food, sitting down a short distance from anyone else.

"Do not worry, Niallen is not too frightening once you have known him for long." The woman, who Asman assumed was Dahlia, smiled and sat down next to him.

"I am technically a prisoner. It would be wise to treat me like one, or else I will begin to think I am one of you." Asman spoke with a flat voice as he stared at the stew.

It seemed like good stew, but with the pain in both his heart and shoulder, he did not feel the need to eat.

"If you prove yourself, perhaps you will end up being one of us. Niallen only keeps you here by force for the safety of Isadren and his people." Dahlia shrugged and Asman glanced to her with furrowed brows.

"I do not wish to be held anywhere against my will, not at any point." Asman huffed gently, the woman nodded understandingly.

"It was just a thought." She said with a small smile. "Eat and rest, we leave very early in the morning."

Asman did not say anything as she stood and left, walking off towards one of the fires and sitting down next to a few men.

The sky was dark, which only slightly surprised Asman, seeing as he did not know when he woke up just a short while ago.

He did end up forcing the stew into his stomach with his mind supplying an alternative of singing a song instead of thinking about his brothers death and who was around him.

Asman was not especially tired, but once the sun set and the people of the camp quieted, it was easier to slip asleep.

He rolled onto his stomach and used his right forearm as a pillow before drifting off without fanfare.

Chapter Two: Wood

Asman did not end up sleeping throughout the night.

Around midnight, he woke to his shoulder sore and burning. He tried to go back to sleep but could not find a position that did not result in more pain.

Eventually, he became frustrated enough to sigh and snatch the fur from the ground before walking to the small tree that was growing singularly in the clearing.

When he was a boy, he would climb the trees just outside the village and stay there when he was upset.

After their father died, he had probably stayed in one of the trees outside Thamor for a few days on end, only coming down to use the restroom or when Sam became irritated enough to force him down to eat.

Now, it seemed perfectly logical to climb this tree and stay in it as long as he could before his 'captors' awoke.

It would have been easy to leave during the night. No one tied him or was watching him, so he just as easily could have ran off and did what he liked.

Asman had thought about it, but decided he was a tad bit frightened to go off in the woods during the night now. The tree was close enough to the few fires for Asman to be able to see the branches as he maneuvered his body up.

The pain in his shoulder was quickly becoming more of a nuisance than anything; a few short hisses at a particularly painful movement, or a pause when Asman felt a stitch pull was only a slight deterrent to climbing the branches.

He had only gone to the first large branch and the lowest. The tree was small enough that if he went further up the branches would have been too thin to stand on.

Asman exhaled lowly as he settled his right shoulder against the tree, the fur draped across his lap but doing hardly nothing to stifle the cold of the night.

He stared off for awhile, looking off at the fireflies that blinked against the long clearing grass.

It only took a short while after that for him to break down crying.

He was alone. Not only at the moment in the tree, but in general, he had no one left.

His mother, his father, his brother; all his family, and even the few friends he had, were all dead and not coming back.

Asman stifled his sobs with his hand, so if anyone awoke during the night, or was even still awake from before, they would not hear him drowning in sadness while sitting in a tree.

Before everything had happened, he would rarely think of such depressing things; but now al he could think about was how much he felt he should be dead along with his family.

Why was he the only one to survive? Were there anymore citizens that lived, or was he truly the last one of them?

It was not until he could see the moon through some of the lower branches that he finally could not cry anymore without fear of his skull bursting from pressure.

He had recounted every good or bad memory with his brother while crying, and eventually Asman let his sobs die down while his hand fell from his mouth.

The moon glistened against wet skin while he wiped the tears away; there was a calmness that fell over the land which calmed him enough to move on. The owls and foxes kept his ears listening while his heartbeat returned to a steady one.

Yet, even if he had exhausted all the terrible thoughts in his system, there was still much to think about.

Asman was never taught much in school; only the basics of mathematics and history. As a child he had a fondness for learning more about both the Feliasian and Isadrenian history.

The books he had borrowed from his teacher were heavily biased to that of Felias but what else would you expect from a village within that kingdom.

The war between Isadren and Felias had only started in Asman's teens. Since he was now just exiting his twenty-sixth summer, the war had been a large part of his life.

Isadrenians were told as being brutes and barbarians, coming from the north with their tales of multiple gods and magic wielding citizens.

Asman had never cared about gods or one god. He had only ever thought of his job and brother and village. There had never been evidence of a higher power, so he did not often dwell on it.

The war had only begun because supposedly, Isadrenians attacked the southern kingdom for no reason. They only wanted blood and carnage.

The books were focused on portraying Isadren as a cold and violent kingdom with insane residents and their head in the clouds. Asman believed the books for a large portion of his life, though several years ago, a merchant came to the village and told Asman of the real truth.

The man was not biased to either of the countries, and only did what he had to do to live as he traveled between the two kingdoms. He only stayed for half a fortnight, but Asman was in awe of the mans words.

That same man had also been the first that Asman had ever been sexual with.

He had only had sex two times before, both with women whom he tried to have a relationship with, but the girls soon realized he was not exactly interested in being romantic with them. Asman had no qualms on having sex with a woman, but to marry one or live his life with one did not appeal to him the same way that men did.

This was yet another thing the Isadrenians were known for, according to the merchant.

Isadren did not care whether or not you married a woman or man. Once Asman heard this he had asked every merchant or bard or tradesman for tales or stories of the northern kingdom that would not judge him for wanting a relationship with a man.

Felias was against people like Asman only just enough that if he were to say he did not want to marry a woman, he would have been shunned from the village and sent to live somewhere else.

It was surreal, finally getting to meet a group of the people he had heard so much yet so little about. But he had also let that wonder and interest dwindle as the years went by.

He had a job and task that needed to be done. There was no time for reading as you tend cattle and chickens, butchering and portioning all day until the sun sank low and you slept through to a new day of doing the same thing.

Asman could admit that perhaps he was staying with the Blood Guards not because of his fear for the dark, but for a wonder of what the people are like.

He could find out so much more truth; Why did the war really start? How did these people live their life? How many gods did they truly worship? Would life be worth living if it meant he could live how he wanted to?

These thoughts were all racing throughout his head, all the way until the sun was rising and pushing the moon down beneath the horizon. Asman was tired and wondered what would happen if he refused to walk all day towards Stelai. He could not even find himself wanting to climb down the tree.

When the sun breached the edge of the forest for the first time, the light shined right over the clearing and the group of people.

Asman watched as they all woke and even flinched a smile when Dahlia found where he had previously been in the campsite and looked around wildly to find where he had gone.

Dahlia frantically asked anyone nearby if they had seen him, at least, that's what he assumed since he could not hear what she was actually saying.

Eventually, the woman ran a stressed hand through her hair and stepped into Niallen's tent.

Asman only barely felt bad for making the woman stress. After all, they had done a poor job of keeping him in one place. You would have thought if they needed his story so badly they would have at least kept an eye or two on him.

The amusement that Asman had felt before quickly turned to curiosity when Niallen stepped out of the tent, his face irritated as if this was just an inconvenience; which it likely was.

There was no smile on Asman's face as he watched Niallen sniff at the air. There certainly was not any glimpse of a smirk when the leaders eyes honed in on the tree Asman was still sitting in as if it was no difficult task to find Asman just by scent.

Asman watched with a tilt to his head as Niallen stalked over toward the tree with an annoyed and slightly angry expression.

"Why are you in a tree, Asman?" Niallen asked as he finally stopped just below the branch.

Asman glanced down at the man before looking towards the fur on his lap and where his hands were fiddling with the soft exterior.

"Because I am." Asman shrugged. "Why? Does it bother you? I feel as though if you wanted me to stay where I was, there could have been better measures put in place."

"I felt as though we had reached an understanding."

"Oh? Had we? I was not aware. No, I was under the impression that I was the prisoner who you are dragging north. After all, you only did focus on the fact that I do not want to go to Isadren." Asman raised an eyebrow as he sent another look to the man.

"You are not a prisoner as long as you do not resist when we travel." Niallen sighed softly. "Why would you not want to go to Isadren? It is not as if there is anywhere else to go. You yourself said you are no longer Feliasian."

"Isadren is cold."

Niallen barked out a laugh at that. Asman stifled a grin at the sound; it felt nice to make someone laugh.

"Yes, it is cold. But you learn to like the cold." Niallen started and crossed his arms. "I would like to leave sometime soon, if you would so please come down from the tree."

Asman exhaled slowly and frowned. It would hurt if he came down no doubt.

He gave one last low sigh before tossing the fur off of his legs and onto the ground in front of Niallen, his bare feet landing in crunchy sun dried grass.

The drop from the lowest branch and the ground was hardly high enough for any chance of a bone breaking, and Asman, seeing as he had done so before, thought it would be quickest for him to jump down.

Even though he knew his wound would likely flare up at the impact, Asman took a deep breath and jumped anyway.

He landed on his feet easily, but he was correct in the laceration sending a sharp pain through his shoulder.

Asman inhaled quickly, but did not yell. He only clenched his teeth and shut his eyes as he breathed through the pain.

"I will have our healer look at your wound again. The cut was deep and there will be a chance of infection if we do not treat it and get you a shirt that covers." Niallen spoke up while Asman breathed.

"I am fine." Asman gritted out before taking one more deep inhale and opening his eyes, not sparing a glance to Niallen and then taking off towards the camp, leaving the man and the fur still standing there.

The members of the camp had already been packing as soon as they woke, but while Asman's brief interruption, they had gotten together most of the things that littered the camp and there was now a herd of horses that these things were putting strapped to.

Every horse seemed to have its owner, and they varied in species and color. Asman had never really been near horses, so he steered clear as best he could of the large animals.

In the village, there had only ever been a donkey or mule being used for work. The only time he had ever even seen a horse was when one pulled the cart of a trader; and when the army had attacked the village.

With the introduction of horses in the camp, came flies, and the flies sometimes did not prefer the horse manure, but Asman's shoulder and wound.

He was constantly trying to wave a hand behind his back while he waited, but after only a few times of him almost tearing the stitches, he finally growled in annoyance and turned his tunic so that the back was in the front. The back being the side that held a huge tear in the cloth and blood staining the edges.

This seemed to deter the flies enough, and it did feel nice for his wound to be covered. But, there was now a gaping slit against the right side of his chest, exposing it and letting anyone who wished look at his skin.

Asman had never been the type to be self conscious. Not when the entirety of his village was either ill-mannered or ugly or literally ill. Asman was actually one of the attractive ones and that was saying something.

Short mousy brown hair and brown eyes, his figure lean with just enough muscle to be able to lift a larger chunk of meat and not able to grow chest or facial hair even though he was past his teen years. Sam used to joke that he got all the genes for hair, since his beard was long and full by the time he was twenty.

Asman hated that he could not grow any hair, but he was still okay with his appearance. Though now, he was surrounded by people who were all attractive in their own way.

The women were athletic and shapely, and even some had short hair that perfectly matched their features.

Some of the men were tall and thick with strength, with long and braided hair or beards that had Asman staring for far too long.

Other men were lean and young, and yet they still had muscled arms and legs that showed through easily beneath the thin tunics slowly being covered by thick leather armor.

Asman was practically drooling over the men within the camp, and the fact they were all carrying some sort of weapon was strangely a turn on for him.

It was not until the Blood Guards began mounting their horses that Asman finally snapped from his wonder and joined the group, ready to walk beside them. He was not particularly surprised that he had to walk, he felt that he would slow them down but he was not angry either; not about that at least.

Asman liked walking, and the day was nice though a little warm. His only worry was that he was perhaps dehydrated enough that if he did not drink then he would be too lethargic to walk.

Though, when Niallen finally mounted his own horse and they began walking, Asman followed behind and listened to the sounds of the forest as they left the clearing.

Chapter Three: Air

Asman was hot, even though there was a steady breeze and the sun was behind the clouds, he was hot.

The lack of water in his system was likely the reason for this; or maybe it was fever from his wound, also seeing as it was leaking hopefully only blood down his back.

He was behind the herd of horses, so nobody could see that he was struggling to keep pace, or stumbling occasionally over a rock. His feet were still without shoes and he barely contained a hiss when a sharp rock would jab into them.

The only reason he knew something was wrong was because he could have walked this distance easily before. Asman was the one to run around the village and gather things for him and Sam, so it was no problem for him to walk long distances.

Now, the horses and him had been walking for a long enough time that the sun was almost directly overhead, and Asman was becoming more and more unstable by the moment.

His stomach boiled and the sweat dripped down his flushed skin onto the edge of his shirt.

When the feeling became too much, he steered off the path just so that when he fell unconscious, it would be in a patch of grass rather than the hard dirt road.

He wondered how long it would take the Guards to know that he was not walking behind him.

Asman did not even reach the grass all the way before his knees were slamming into the ground and his eyes shut, welcoming the darkness.

"Asman. Asman!"

Asman woke by a sharp slap to his cheek, making his eyes snap open and his hand immediately reach up to slap back at the offender.

It was Niallen, so Asman immediately regretted trying to do so; trying, because the man caught his wrist easily.

"You fell unconscious, I only wished to wake you." Niallen said while Asman quickly inhaled and exhaled from the slight scare he got.

He was lying exactly where he had walked to and remembering vaguely falling, but now, the whole group was standing around and watching.

Dahlia was close by and had a worried expression, but she was the only one that held that face. The rest seemed to not care all that much.

"One of your stitches has pulled. Why did you not say? We would have stopped, or allowed you to ride at least." Niallen inquired and let go of Asman's wrist finally.

Asman noticed that his tunic was pulled up slightly, far enough that it was likely someone checking the wound.

He ignored Niallen's question and worked towards sitting up, pulling his tunic down and staring down at where the horses hooves were prancing nervously. Asman did not know much about horses, but he assumed it was the scent of his blood.

"Come, Hilcren will stitch your wound again and I will fetch some water." Niallen sighed and stood from where he had been squatting down next to Asman.

Niallen held out a hand and Asman ignored it, instead using his good hand to push his body back up off the ground.

He hated being wounded, unable to walk without passing out and drawing pity from others. Asman did not need pity, he needed to not have to worry about stitches unraveling and the possibility of infection in his shoulder.

Asman stumbled a bit as he stood, and only let Niallen lead him to another man with a guiding hand on his good shoulder because he did not want another shot of pain if he tried to remove it.

Niallen left him with the other man, who was climbing down from his horse and then reaching into one of the bags.

Asman assumed this was Hilcren, so he only stood there and watched as the man pulled from the bag a needle, spool of thick string, and pair of small scissors.

"Turn around and remove your shirt." Hilcren said with a demanding voice that made Asman do so without objection.

Hilcren was as handsome as the rest of the men, and had short blond hair with small braids in it. He was one of the younger members, without a beard and only slightly shorter than Asman, but still strong enough that the latter did not disobey him.

Asman kept his shirt on his arms, and only showed what he had to of his sides and front.

Hilcren was quick with cleaning the dried blood from around the wound, only careful enough to not open or unravel a stitch, but not careful enough that Asman was not scrunching his face in pain.

While Hilcren cleaned, Niallen came back holding an animal bladder that was likely filled with water.

He handed the bladder over to Asman, and with a stern 'drink.' directed towards him, Asman did so.

The water felt nice filling his stomach and cooling his throat, but he only took a few gulps before trying to hand the bladder back to Niallen.

Niallen only shook his head and pushed the water back towards Asman, tilting his head as if telling the shorter to continue.

Asman did not object to this either, and took a few more long drinks.

He hissed when Hilcren finally stabbed the needle through his skin, pulling the string through one half of the wound to the other. Asman bit his lip harshly when Hilcren tightened the string and pulled the two halves together, tying a knot and then clipping the ends with the scissors.

When he was sure that Hilcren had finished, Asman pulled his shirt back down and took one more drink of water before handing it back to Niallen.

Niallen took the bladder this time and gave a nod to Hilcren prior to leading Asman back towards his his horse.

"You will ride with me until we reach Stelai." Niallen stated easily as he corked the bladder and slid it into its saddlebag.

"There is no need, I will be fine to walk now." Asman shook his head, mostly just wary of being so close to a horse.

"We can walk faster if we do not have to wait for you. My horse is big enough to hold us both, now get on."

Asman opened his mouth to say something but was cut off when Niallen's horse whinnied and shook its head a bit, causing Asman to jump and back away a bit.

"She will not hurt you, Asman. Come, put your foot in the stirrup and your hand here, sit there." Niallen waved to the foot piece and then patted his hand against the cantle of the saddle.

Asman looked at the horse again and sighed before nodding hesitantly, putting his foot and hand where Niallen told him to. He pulled himself up easily, but did not like how the horse stepped a few times to shift her weight.

He shut his eyes and only opened them again once he felt Niallen get up onto the saddle with him.

The larger man slid into the front, and Asman adjusted slightly forwards so that he was more sturdily on the saddle. The cantle separated any awkward touches.

Niallen did not seem to mind the adjustment and only picked up the reins, clicking his tongue and tugging said reins to nudge the horse forward.

As soon as the horse began moving, Asman's heart rate spiked and he inhaled sharply. He grabbed at the back of Niallen's armor on instinct when he felt unsteady.

"You are going to damage the leather if you grip so tightly, just place your hands on my waist." Niallen growled out, seemingly annoyed at where Asman's hands were tangled into the leather.

Asman swallowed harshly and did as told, lightly placing his palms on the mans hips. It only took the horse speeding up slightly for Asman to tighten his grip and shut his eyes again.

That is how he remained for a good portion of the ride; his hands squeezing Niallen's hips and his eyes shut tight while he ignored the rolling in his stomach from all the movements.

At some point, Dahlia came forward next to Asman and tapped his shoulder before handing him a few strips of dried meat.

Asman was hungry, so he ate one of them and kept the rest for later. This was just past noon, and it was not until the sun began to sink beneath the trees that the stench of a village floated through the air.

There was distinct smell that came from the animals and people living in a village or town that Asman was used to. Though, he had come to better like the smell of the forest rather than manure and smoke.

Asman opened his eyes when they reached the gates of Stelai and Niallen called out to a postman that he and the Guards were just traveling west and were in hope of restocking their supplies.

Surprisingly, the man above the gate did not question Niallen. Asman furrowed his brows and looked back to the Guards only to find that they have hidden their swords and axes beneath blankets and cloaks. They still looked as if they were a small army, but perhaps the guard did not care that much.

Stelai was a bigger village; a city if you will. It had quite a lot of people roaming the streets and vendors lining the cobblestone streets.

Asman had never visited Stelai before, but had heard of it from his merchant.

He was looking around constantly, his eye catching on almost everything that it could; a vendor selling jewelry, another one selling bright red and green apples, and all the people walking around as if one of their neighboring villages was not attacked by their own kingdom.

Asman hardly noticed as the first tear slipped down his face; whether it was in sadness or anger, he did not care. He only let go of Niallen to wipe it away before returning his hand.

This city was just like Thamor before they were all killed and burned. It was alive and thriving, with children running through the streets and the sound of men's laughter coming from the tavern, if not a little larger than his hometown.

Their houses were still built, there was no blood littering the streets, no sounds of screaming and crying. There was only a normal city, unaware of all around it, and the people inside of it living through the day and to the next.

It was an unexpected anger within Asman; seeing these people so freely remain in a kingdom where their own guards attack and kill them.

He wanted to scream at them, tell them to leave while they could and ensure that their children would not be killed. Yell at them that Felias was wrong about so many things and that were just waiting there like lambs to the slaughter.

"Asman. I would prefer to not have bruises on my hips for the next week if you would be so kind to let go."

Asman released the grip he did not know he had at Niallen's quiet hiss. Instead, he removed his hands and placed them at his own thighs.

The people in the streets made way for the nearly thirty horses making their way to the stable, and when they arrived, each rider dismounted their horse and let them be taken away for the night. Everyone retrieved their valuables from their horse before crowding outside as they waited.

When it came time for Asman to dismount, he let Niallen do so first before swinging his legs to one side and hopping down. He was pleased to note that the pain was not as sharp as it was with the tree that morning. The cobblestone actually felt nice against his feet.

Niallen allowed a stable hand to take the mare before giving the boy a Feliasian coin and walking back out of the building.

Asman followed close by as to not get lost in the steady stream of people returning home for the night.

Niallen led Asman and the Guards to an inn, likely the only one large enough to have the amount of rooms they needed.

Luckily, there were only a few patrons already there, so when the whole Guard stepped in, it was only a tad crowded.

Asman watched as each Guard got a room, some asking for one that housed two people instead of one, and some asking for only one bed for two people. Overall, the men and women seemed to be coin efficient in a sense, not caring whether or not they had to share.

He also noticed that Niallen allowed the rest of the Guard to get rooms before he did. They were the last ones in the group left once the rest went to find their rooms and get situated.

Niallen asked for a room with two beds and handed over the coin while the innkeeper slid a key towards Niallen. Asman only kept quiet and hugged the rolled fur that Niallen had told him to carry, following the man up the stairs and into their room; he hoped no one noticed his lack of shoes still as they walked.

The room was normal, and larger than what Asman was used to at home. The only notable features being a desk, a small table in between the two small beds, and a medium sized mirror on the wall.

Niallen immediately shut the door behind them and then took the bed closest to that door, setting his bags down on it before turning back to Asman.

"You will stay here for tonight, I have some things to attend to so I will not be back until later." Niallen announced swiftly. "Please do not leave and find a tree tonight. Dahlia will bring you food."

Asman huffed softly and nodded, watching as Niallen exited the room not a few seconds after they entered.

As the door shut, Asman sighed and walked over to his bed, tossing the fur to the side before stripping his shirt off and sitting down while facing the mirror.

He grimaced as he turned and maneuvered his body to see the wound, all red and scabbed over. Ugly, to give it a word.

Asman did not bother to put his shirt back on and only laid down on his stomach on the bed, sighing at the feeling of a mattress beneath him instead of the ground.

The sun was shining in through the window, making lines as the rays shined onto the floor in between the beds.

Asman was tired, but he figured he had better wait for Dahlia to bring him food, since he was also slightly hungry too. He hoped there was at least some water coming with the meal also; though, if not, there was Niallen's water that was resting with his things on the bed over.

So, Asman laid in the bed and watched as the sunlight became smaller and smaller, until it was finally gone and the room was lit only by the remnants of the light of day.

When Dahlia finally arrived with a plate of bland tasting stew and a cup of ale, he thanked her and then sat down to eat. She only said for him to have a good night and then left off to her own room.

Asman ate in silence and drank down the ale before setting the bowl and cup outside the door and lying back down, this time, allowing himself to fall asleep.

He was quick to do so, with his belly full and his body warm from the ale. He only partly left the blanket on his lower half because of that warmth.

If he was tired enough to think he was at home, it would never be shared to anyone but himself.

Chapter Four: Earth

I t was Niallen that woke him the next morning, only saying Asman's name multiple times and then stating that some of the Guard were going to resupply and that Asman was to stay in the room until they returned.

Asman, being freshly woken up, only mumbled an agreement and went back to sleep after hearing the door open and close.

He did not know how long he slept after that, but he later woke up to Dahlia coming into the room and dropping off a bit of bread and jam.

Dahlia stayed while he ate and even if they did not talk, it was still nice to not be alone.

The bread was good and fresh, and the jam was sweet and tasted of mulberries. It certainly filled his stomach nicely, and made him feel overall better about his situation.

Sure, his whole family was dead and he was being taken to Isadren by a group of scary and attractive people, but at least they fed him sweet jam and made sure he was not dying.

Soon enough, Dahlia finally broke the silence by asking how his shoulder was feeling.

Asman furrowed his brows and gently rolled his shoulder, only to find that there was little to no pain. It was barely a dull ache, more so from sleeping strange than there being a large laceration there.

When he turned to look in the mirror to check the wound, he only found a scar sitting in the place where the cut had once been. Even the stitches were gone, and as he looked, he found them littering the bed. His mood spited almost immediately.

"What the fuck? Dahlia, what is this?" Asman asked with a panicked tilt, his hand coming to rub at the tip of the scar.

"Fae magic." She said gently and took the plate from where it was drooping in Asman's hand. "Niallen thought it best that your wound was healed for our journey. It is only trouble when you deal with such an injury while traveling."

Asman exhaled shakily and turned back to the woman, eyeing her with an incredulous look.

"How... Why would he do this? I was fine dealing with the wound. It kept me- It kept me grounded. I needed that wound, that was all I had to remind myself that I was not left unscathed in the attack." Asman huffed sharply and glanced down at the floor, tears gathering in his eyes. "I deserved that wound. It was- I cannot-."

Asman's breathing quickened as he continued to clutch at the scar. His only reason for allowing himself to live, gone, in just a night.

"Asman. Breath. You did not deserve that wound, it was painful, and nobody deserved what had happened to your village no more than you deserve to be in pain. There is a scar still, this will remind you of those who died, and how they would have wanted you to live. You survived, Asman. But that wound did not prove anything more than Felias is corrupt." Dahlia stated sternly as she sat down beside Asman, blocking his view of the mirror.

"I do not care. I wanted the pain. I should have died with my brother and the pain was my punishment for watching him die and then running like a coward." Asman cried out as hot tears slipped down his face.

"You ran on instinct. Because you ran, you will be able to get revenge on Felias. The gods have done this for a reason, Asman; you were meant to live and to tell the story of your village."

Asman sobbed angrily and stood, shaking his head and picking up his shirt from where it had fallen.

"I do not want to tell a story. I want to go home. I want to see my brother alive and only have to worry about whether or not the fence on the cow pen in sturdy enough." Asman frowned as his lip wobbled. "I never wanted to be involved with a war, or have to go to Isadren just to tell a story about my village being slaughtered to a Queen who could not give a shite about it."

Asman finally pulled the tunic back over his head, this time with the hole on his back again, before scrubbing his hands over his face and leaving Dahlia in the room alone.

He slammed the door behind him and quickly made his way down the stairs, ignoring the curious glances from the Guard members sitting at the tables on the Inns main floor.

Asman did not know where he was going, but for now, all he wanted to do was find a tree and get away from the damn Blood Guard and their asshole leader.

"Asman! Where are you going, Asman?"

Said man growled as the target of his anger appeared, followed by only a dozen of the Guard.

Asman ignored Niallen and continued walking, dodging the people in the street as he headed for the gates. Unfortunately, he was not fast enough, and Niallen laid a hand on his shoulder to stop Asman.

Immediately, Asman turned around and punched as hard as he could into Niallen's cheek.

Niallen grunted and stepped backwards as the hit landed, the man lifting a hand to wipe the small trickle of blood that dropped from the corner of his mouth.

Asman did not even say as to why he did it, and only continued his trek towards the gate. He only got a few steps before arms were wrapping around his shoulders and picking him up.

He struggled in what was likely Niallen's arms before getting angry enough to smash his head backwards until it connected with Niallen's nose; as Niallen let go, Asman quickly shifted his arm down to clasp at the pommel of the mans sword peaking from his cloak.

Asman still had tears running down his face as he backed away and held the sword up. He would be damned if he let Niallen think that just because he was previously compliant, it did not in the least mean that he was weak.

"You had no right, Niallen." Asman whispered harshly, then throwing the sword to the ground and walking off again. This time no one followed.

Asman lost himself in the crowd and with the sharp turns, he knew that even if the Blood Guards were following him before, he had lost them.

He did not try for the gate anymore and instead just swiftly walked around the city, listening to the bards and troubadours that were placed sporadically throughout the courtyards.

The townspeople were luckily too focused on the song or their own errands rather than his disheveled shirt and bare feet.

Asman eventually found a small pond in a yard that held no song and sat down at the edge of the water.

He sighed softly and scrubbed a hand over his face, listening to the people walking by with swift steps.

"Excuse me? Are you going to sing, or is this spot open?"

Asman looked up at the young man who had spoke to him, hands clutched around a lute and soft blond hair covered with a feathered hat.

"No, no, go ahead and sing." Asman waved a hand and gave a small smile, if only to show he was not a crotchety old man.

"Thank you." The boy smiled back and bowed, but did not immediately start singing.

Instead, he sat down next to Asman and took off his hat just to set it on the ground in front of him.

"You seem a bit down, sir. I would like to play my next ballad in comradery with your melancholy." The bard stated as he strummed a few light notes. "What is it that makes you so melancholic?"

Asman glanced over at the man briefly and shook his head with a sigh.

"Death, and ignorance. Guilt." Asman said, shrugging his shoulders lightly.

The bard nodded and cleared his throat, quickly forming a melody with his lute and tying together the pointless chords he had played previously.

"Over the hillI will be waiting on for youI won't pretendThat you don't mean nothing to meCome now, come now,Come back now, come back now."

Asman frowned as he recognized the song that the bard was singing. The soft melody had been sung before in his village from one of the traveling bards.

"The doubt will creepAnd crawl in on youThe dark can leapAnd fall upon youCome back now, come back now."

The bard had a very nice voice, and Asman could feel himself shutting his eyes and letting more tears fall as he sang.

"Let it be, let it go,Let it fall, let it blowLet it come, let it go,Let it fall, we will know."

The bard finished with a final strum of the sad lute strings. Asman still cried even as the sound dissipated in the yard.

He stayed doing so even as the bard clapped him softly on the back and set a few coins onto Asman's leg. The bard did not say more before launching into a more jaunty tune, not anything like what he had played previously.

Asman sighed deeply once more before wiping his tears and gathering the coin, standing and walking off back into the city with the sound of the bards lute at his back.

It did not take long for him to be intercepted my a Guard.

The man was one that he had seen before, but did not know who he was. He was one of the ones with the long beard and large bodies, dark skin that glistened in the sun; Asman did not resist when the man picked him up and threw him over his shoulder.

Asman thought this method was a bit much, but assumed that he was a prisoner now and likely would be treated as such.

After he was hauled over the mans shoulder, said man made his way back towards the inn, where Asman was sure Niallen was angry at him.

The people in the streets did not seem to mind the fact of Asman's position, but Asman did. He had certain partialities during sex that were not exactly gentle in nature.

This man, even though Asman was sure he was not attempting to, was very easily piquing those interests with how he was handling Asman. It took all of the smaller mans will to not get an erection and keep the redness in his face to a minimum.

He instead thought of what Niallen was going to do when the man brought him back; was he going to punch him as payback? Or shackle him and make Asman seem more like a prisoner? Maybe

Niallen would just forget the whole situation and kill Asman for head butting him.

Either way, it made Asman slightly nervous, and also angry.

He had been telling the truth when he said Niallen had no right. Asman had wanted to heal from that wound on his own and make it a reminder of his survival and his brothers death.

Niallen had taken his choice away and Asman was pissed. The larger man had deserved that punch and head butt; Asman also felt proud that he could make the man bleed and steal his sword when Niallen was supposed to be the leader of the 'Blood Guard' and reported to the Queen of Isadren.

Perhaps this is why Niallen also looked furious as the man carrying him shoulder Asman off of him and onto the ground.

Asman grunted as he hit the ground in front of the inn, where the Guard and Niallen were all standing with varying looks.

The only person who did not have an angry or negative face was Dahlia, who in Asman's opinion, looked almost smug.

Asman ignored all the dangerous looks in favor of gritting his teeth and sneering at Niallen.

"How is your nose?" Asman asked, which only seemed to irritate Niallen.

"I tried to be kind, Asman. I fed you and saved your life and even after that I decided to use valuable fae magic to rid you of your wound. You should be thankful, yet you only respond with violence and selfishness." Niallen frowned, Asman could see the stain where he had not wiped the blood completely from his lip.

"You did this of your own volition. I never asked for any of this and will not act as if I appreciate things that I do not. If you did not want me here, then you should have left me." Asman stated, his voice surprisingly calm for all the tension surrounding him.

He was still on the ground, but he had raised himself so he was on his knees instead of his arse.

"You know why I did not leave you. Again, I tried to be kind to you, but you seem intent on behaving like a prisoner even though you did not have to be one."

"So I am one now then. You see that the only way that you will be able to yank someone somewhere against their will is by force." Asman kept Niallen's gaze just like the day prior; as if it was a fight. "I hope that the next time you forcefully take another from their home, you are smart enough to realize what you are actually doing."

"What is it that you believe I am actually doing?" Niallen asked with furrowed brows.

"Confirming the rumors." Asman stated simply. "The rumors that Isadrenians have no regard for emotion. They only take what they want and will do what they must to win; even if it means killing innocent people to do so."

"We do not kill if there is not a need. Those tales were told by our enemy and a depraved kingdom. You have agreed that Felias is corrupt, why do you resist now?"

"Who is to say I am resisting? I am only upset that you have made my choices for me. I know how this ends. Do you, Niallen?"

"What do you mean? Of course I know what will happen; we will return to Isadren and you will tell your story to the Queen." Niallen seemed irritated at Asman's question.

"You are foolish to think that is all. Do you believe that your Queen will allow a Feliasian to live in Isadren after I have said my piece? She will kill me, and I am only trying to speed up my inevitable demise. I should have died with my brother, but I will die soon anyways."

Niallen bristled at this, and even the Guard seemed to be uneasy at Asman's words.

Nobody spoke for a moment, and the only sound was that of the city; Asman was surprised that no one especially cared about the encounter happening in front of the inn.

Eventually, Niallen spoke, and Asman was left wanting to strangle the man.

"Asman is not our prisoner. Jacksill, tell the stable hand to begin prepping our horses."

Chapter Five: Dark

"Niallen, that was not the point of this conversation!" Asman yelled, wholly confused as to how the man still could say he was not a prisoner.

"Why would I keep you prisoner? You said that you were not resisting, correct?" Niallen inquired with a shrug towards Asman.

"I meant I would not resist to be a prisoner. I told you that you would have to keep me as one if you intended on taking me anywhere." Asman huffed and waved his hands out in front of him.

"You have been willing before this, why do you need to be shackled this time?"

Asman paused and stayed quiet at that. He knew the reason, but was not keen on tell Niallen.

"Do not be stupid, Niallen." He said instead, hoping that if he insulted the man that maybe he would get the hint. "I could run off again, or punch you again, or steal your sword. Again."

Niallen sighed and shut his eyes for a moment, rubbing his temples before waving to one of the Guards.

"Tie him up. If he wants to be a prisoner so bad, then so be it."
Niallen said and then walked off in the direction of the stables.

Asman exhaled lowly, more of a sigh of relief than anything. Dahlia
gave him a strange look as one of the Guards stepped forward, pulling
a loop of rope from his belt.

He let himself be tied with his hands in front of him. Although he
was upset with his wound being gone, it also felt a lot better to not
be in pain constantly.

The rough dealings that the man in charge of him put him through
did nothing more than make a slight flush appear, though he was sure
that no one noticed.

It seemed that the Guard had already collected their things and
resupplied, with some new satchels and bags added to the many
others.

Asman was walked through the streets by a hand on his arm,
not kind but not gentle either. He understood that they might be
rougher now, but the way the man was just bringing in the edge of
harshness was almost annoying Asman; if he was to be a prisoner,
they should treat him as such.

Luckily, the hand let go when they reached the stables. The man
only nudged him towards Niallen again, who was loading his horse
slowly.

Niallen glanced at Asman with an arched brow and tugged the final
strap of leather down before turning to the smaller man and sighing
once more; Asman felt as if the man was doing a lot of that lately.

"This is what you wanted then? To be tied up and helpless instead of free and able?" Niallen questioned while taking one of Asman's arms in his hand and pulling him towards the horse.

"I am not helpless. You can attest, I have a thick skull." Asman huffed and did what he hoped Niallen was pointing him to by slipping his foot into the stirrup.

Asman pulled himself up as best he could without the full use of his hands, only grabbing what he could and sliding up into the saddle for the second time.

Niallen was quick to mount also, but this time went behind Asman and got comfortable there instead of in front of him.

"In more ways then one apparently." Was all Niallen said as he picked up the reins and boxed Asman's body in.

Asman assumed the change in position was so that he would not fall, seeing as he could no longer hold onto Niallen's waist with how close his hands were tied together.

He clicked his tongue at Niallen's comment and only placed his hands on the leather horn at the front of the saddle. Asman had to admit that this position was far more comfortable than being in the back.

Asman was still uncomfortable around the horse, but at least he could pet the mare for comfort and perhaps earn some favor with her.

Though, even if Asman was petting her, she did not seem to notice and only started to walk forward when Niallen made the noise that required her to do so.

Niallen led them through the city after paying the stable master, but rather than go through the gate they had entered through, Niallen steered the mare down the streets and north towards what was likely another gate.

Asman was right, and by near noon they were back on the road north.

The return to the forest was nice, and even though he was tied at the wrists, Asman felt more secure than the day before.

Riding was the same, though. The sound of hooves hitting the dirt and birds singing was almost identical to yesterday.

Asman only stared ahead and played little games in his head like; how long will it take to reach that patch of wildflowers? Or, listening to bird calls to see which are different or the same. His favorite, was seeing how long he could hum until someone told him to stop. This was the current one.

At first, he had started out with little tunes he had heard before, but once he had run out of songs, he only made little melodies that did not amount to anything.

The little games distracted him from reality, and let him break away from a bit. It felt good to not think of anything bad, only the sounds of the horses, the forest, and himself to calm the painful storm in his mind.

The feeling of the rope on his wrists and the horses mane under his fingers was something that grounded him; not unlike how the wound had.

Having the wound healed made him sad only because it was a reminder, but Dahlia was right that there was still a scar. So maybe Asman was more upset at how quickly Niallen had decided to use magic on him without asking.

Asman was brought up to believe magic was evil, and only ever did harm to those who used it or were affected by it. Like a lot of things told to him by other Feliasians, the Blood Guard had proved that this specific rumor was not true.

Asman almost felt bad for telling Niallen that the man was confirming rumors when even Asman himself knew that he was rather destroying them. The Guard had not killed anyone so far, and had only been nice. Besides when Niallen had choked Asman, it was the latter who had been the most violent.

Of course, he still hated that Niallen had healed his wound without saying he was going to do so. There could have been a warning or at least a question of what Asman wanted, but no one get as if they cared of his opinion.

No one cared that his village was dead, except maybe Dahlia. She had been the only one to talk to him with empathy. Asman lost his brother and home, and nobody had even once asked him if he was alright.

He knew that he was not close with these people, but it was the least they could after stealing him away and taking him to the fucking arctic tundra that was Isadren.

It was this fact that held him back from sharing what he was actually thinking. He was being petty, but felt that if Niallen wanted to know what he was thinking, then he could ask with a little more emotion than annoyance.

Asman, throughout the day, likely thought about more things than he ever had before. He was bored and desperately wanted to talk, but decided he had too much pride to do that.

The Guards were talking to each other, so he at least got a few bits of entertainment from that.

Some would talk about how glad they were that they were finally going home; evidently the Guards had been gone for nearly a year.

There was discussion of what they would do when they returned, most of them saying they missed their families, though some said they only longed for staying in one place for more than a day.

Asman listened to as much as he could, and even if he felt a bit odd eavesdropping on other peoples personal lives, it gave him something to do.

Niallen was remaining silent, so it was not as if Asman could talk to anyone else. The man seemed hell bent on being the first in the group to walk down the road, and that meant that the two of them were a fair bit away from the rest.

Even Dahlia was talking and laughing from behind them. The other women talking about things like seeing their husbands or children again.

One of the women and men were married and had left their child with his grandmother for the duration of the campaign. Asman felt bad that they had gone so long from their child.

The talking only continued as they stopped by a river to give the horses a rest and water.

Asman was kept sitting on a rock while the rest of the group sat around and laughed some more.

He sighed gently and leaned his head on his knees, his wrapped hands dangling in front of his ankles as his body folded in half.

When it came time to leave, Niallen dragged him up and onto the mare once again after handing him a strip of meat; Asman had ate the other two while waiting to fall asleep last night.

They walked until nightfall, or rather the horses walked and Asman sat there bored, tired, and his arse aching.

The Guards drew camp a fair bit off the road near a creek and after tying the horses. Asman was tied to a tree just the same as the animals.

He was at least confined loose enough that he could lie down if he wanted, his hands being the only thing wrapped as a single rope looped around the tree.

Asman did eventually lie down, but only after he was handed a few more strips of meat and Dahlia let him drink the rest of her canteen, though it did not have much in it.

"Why did you do this, Asman?" Dahlia asked as he took a large swig from said canteen.

He did not respond at first, and chewed and swallowed a bite of meat before actually speaking.

"There was too much trust. Niallen thought too quickly that I was to be trusted, and I feel that is not a good trait during a war."

"He felt bad for you; and I can admit that he did seem to trust you quicker than most. We do not usually hold people prisoner. Especially those who have gone through what you have." Dahlia sat down next to Asman against the tree.

"It was foolish and I do not need anyone to pity me. I should have not let you all take me so easily." Asman glanced down to the ground and tore off another chunk of meat just so that he did not continue to talk.

"Why not? You would have come with us either way, so it was smarter to be willing rather than be tied. Though, I suppose you did this for a separate reason, did you not?"

Asman did not spare a glance to the woman and only harshly swallowed the food in his mouth.

Dahlia might have been the only one to speak to him without malice, but she also seemed to pick up on what Asman was truly thinking faster too.

"I realize you believe it is unwise to leave someone who does not want to go somewhere untied, but perhaps you also are more willing than you want to be?" Dahlia tilted her head a little and continued to look at Asman, who was still staring at the ground.

Asman exhaled softly and played a bit with the rope on his wrist; it was beginning to become uncomfortable after wearing it for the whole day.

"If I leave willingly, I am leaving behind my brother. I am throwing my whole village away just to run and never look back again."

Dahlia stayed silent momentarily, letting what Asman said sink in.

"What was there to throw away? What reason was there for you to stay? Would you have returned there and subjected yourself to that pain again?" Dahlia questioned with a slight shrug. "Just because you have found a place to go does not mean you are disrespecting their memory, you are prolonging it by telling their stories."

"Do you honestly believe I have a life to live in Isadren?" Asman finally looked to Dahlia, his brows furrowed. "If I survive your Queen, what would I do? Live alone, with no family or friends to speak of and previous affiliations with the kingdom yours hates?"

"People in Isadren are far more understanding than you have been taught to believe, Asman. We understand what unfairness and ignorance that your King has instilled in your kingdom; there are plenty of Isadrenians that have left Felias and fled to Isadren. We accepted them and if you wanted, you would be no different."

Asman let Dahlias words ring out while he sighed and leaned his head back against the tree.

If he allowed himself to be taken to Isadren, there were many things that were up in the air to him. Dahlia could not know everyone's opinions.

Thinking that he would be okay if he was suddenly placed within an Isadrenian village would only give Asman false hope. Certainly every Isadrenian would not be so quick to accept him as a prior Feliasian.

Felias has destroyed so many of their towns, villages, and cities. They have killed so many of their people, and Asman was not ignorant to the fact that people would see him as only a Feliasian.

He would still be alone, without Sam, in a foreign land and wondering what would come next.

Would, if he allowed himself to freely walk with the Guards, they see him as only a Feliasian?

Had he truly been taken against his will, or had he only made it seem like that so he would not feel so horrible about leaving his village to burn?

Asman hated not knowing the things that were happening with his own mind. He wanted to know why he felt as if he could walk with the Guards and be fine.

He wanted to know why Niallen saw fit to trust him so quickly when there was no reason to.

He needed to know why he saw fit to trust Niallen so quickly. Asman knew the man would not hurt him, but why?

Chapter Six: Light

After Asman and Dahlia had spoke, the prior had finished the dried meat and then went to bed all without talking to the woman again.

There was much to think about in his opinion.

It was likely not ideal that he spent most of the night awake and doing such. It was far past midnight when his mind finally calmed, but he felt notably better about what in the world was happening.

Come morning, he would have to apologize to Niallen. Not for punching or head butting him, but for making rude comments about Isadrenians, and assuming the worst from the man who had saved his life; even if he did not want him to.

Asman had realized that even if he was tied, he had put himself in this situation and had left his brother. There was no turning back from this point on; even if he had left his brothers body to burn, he would not have anything to turn back for. Isadren was his future at this time, whether or not it meant his death was not something he cared about.

Due to all this thinking that Asman was partaking in, he did not perhaps get the best nights sleep he could have. So when morning actually came, he was tired and maybe a tad touchy when it came to interacting.

He had almost snapped at Dahlia for pulling the rope against his wrists too hard, but at the last second, Niallen had intervened and arrived to steal Asman away to the horses.

Asman mounted the mare with heavy limbs, and when Niallen mounted also, Asman had to fight leaning back against the mans chest and falling asleep.

The morning was warm and dry enough that Asman was almost immediately ready to drift off, though he stopped himself since he still had to apologize to Niallen.

Luckily, he was handed a couple strips of salted and dried fish to snack on and keep him awake by one of the men. That and a few sips from Niallen's water was enough to keep him present until they got on the road once more.

The sun had not fully risen above the tree line when Asman finally put off waiting and spoke.

"Niallen?"

The man hummed questioningly but did not say anything.

"... I am sorry." Asman said eventually. "For the things I said about Isadrenians, and for not appreciating all that you have done for me. Even if I did not want it at the time, you were kind in patching me up and not leaving me for dead. I am sorry I did not say it sooner."

Niallen did not respond for a moment, and Asman sat there awkwardly while the man stayed silent.

Eventually, Niallen hummed again and sighed slightly.

"Does this mean you will be more compliant with going to Isadren?" Niallen asked. "I know that you only reacted as you did because you are mourning. Although I would prefer to let you do as you wish, we need your information for the war."

Asman huffed and rubbed a thumb against the skin beneath the rope.

"If I am not a prisoner, what am I? I will go with you and the Guards voluntarily, but I cannot sit idly by as you march me to my death. I need something to do." Asman stared off to the edge of the road, where the horse he and Niallen were on seemed to be gradually veering towards a bush of Catmint.

Niallen only steered the mare back on the path and went back to his thoughtful silence.

Asman, having already got what he had wanted to say out, focused his efforts on running his fingers through the horses man just as he did yesterday.

He had only ever had one pet, and that was only a stray cat that he would sneak bits of chicken to when Sam was not looking.

Asman had named her Calendula after he had spotted her lying in a thicket of the herb one morning. She ended up disappearing one day, but Asman was not shocked as most stray cats or dogs did so regularly.

He figured he should name the horse, since there was nothing else to do while Niallen speculated on what Asman had said.

The mare was a deep brown color with a tannish mane and tail, so there was not really anything spectacular about her coat that would render a name.

But Asman liked how despite Niallen tugging her reins, she always tried to sneak off to the various wild flowers that were in bloom.

The mare seemed to favor those with more blue or violet flowers. Asman knew deep down that it was unwise to name an animal that was only for transportation; but he landed on Berry anyway. Blueberries seemed the bluest thing he could think of, seeing as he was not all that knowledgeable in the weeds that grew on the side of the road.

Berry, and the other horses, were something that Asman was still slightly frightened by when he was on the ground. But when riding, the only fear was that Niallen would let him fall off Berry's back and get trampled by the other horses.

Though, even for all his worrying, Niallen had not seemed to want to let him get trampled so far; even though Asman had done a fair bit to warrant that reaction.

It still made him worry sometimes.

Near noon, the sky had considerably darkened while the air stayed warm, the clouds were thick enough that there could be rain or there could not be.

Asman could not smell any storms, but the temperature and light levels made it so that he was too tired to care.

He had not gotten a very good nights rest, so while they rode, Asman began to feel himself drifting off occasionally while sitting.

Every movement from Berry was lulling him further and the sounds and light talking coming from the Guards was soothing in a sense.

Asman had shut his eyes and let his head sink down. He barely registered that he had actually fallen asleep until there was a hand splaying across his chest and keeping him up.

He inhaled sharply and pulled his head up, but did not open his eyes and instead just fell back onto Niallen's chest; he figured if the man had a problem than he could move him.

It seemed apparent that Niallen did not have an issue when Asman drifted off again and was not awakened again.

The sleep was unlike what he was used to; Asman faded in and out when a loud noise or he needed to adjust his position slightly. He did not know if he could even call it sleep, but it still left him more rested than before.

He had taken a break for a bit when the scenery became beautiful enough for him to want to see it.

The were riding on a hill, with a sharp cliff face that let them see out over the land.

There was a lake not too far off, hidden in the forest and large enough so there was a small village tucked against one of the bays.

The forest itself was surreal to look at such a height. The tips of the trees were lower than Asman and the Guards, and there was a slight fog or mist over the span of what he could see.

Asman was still against Niallen's chest, but he had turned his head to the left so that he could see over the cliff.

Again, the man did not seem to care about their positions and only made sure to keep Berry from veering too close to the edge. After they had began descending again, Asman shut his eyes once more and fell back into his pseudo sleep.

He did not wake until later on, when the horses had stopped and Niallen finally pushed Asman off his chest.

Asman opened his eyes and caught himself just before he would have fallen onto Berrys neck. He yawned and dismounted from the mare easily, finally taking in where they had stopped.

They were on a riverbank, with a grass field and a one foot drop off to a small strip of sand.

The horses were taken to the river one by one so that they could drink, but some of the animals, including Berry, wandered towards the body of water anyway.

Niallen's tent was set up quickly, and the fires ignited with the same efficiency. Dahlia took the liberty to lead Asman over to the river also; the latter did not appreciate how much he felt like a horse too.

"I thought you might want to rinse off. You have soot and blood on you still." Dahlia said with a sad grimace.

"Oh." Was all he said back, looking down at his hands and feet to find that they were both indeed covered in dirt and the blackish smears associated with charcoal.

"I can untie you for bit and leave you some privacy, but you have to promise not to leave. Niallen has said he will give you better clothes and shoes if you stay here."

Asman briefly looked past Dahlia to see where Niallen had sat by a fire and was helping to slice a few potatoes in his palm.

The man did not seem to notice and only chuckled at something one of the Guard had said. Asman sighed through his nose and nodded at Dahlia.

"I will not go anywhere." He said while holding his wrists up.

Dahlia smiled softly and untied the binds gently, keeping the rope wrapped in a loop loosely around her forearm.

Asman rubbed at his tender skin for a second before reaching to pull his tunic off and avoiding catching anyone's eye.

He hesitated at his trousers as he knew that at least Dahlia was still looking at him.

"You can take them off in the river; you will not be needing them once you get new clothes anyway." Dahlia grinned, seemingly realizing Asman's discomfort. She wordlessly handed him a thin cloth bag that likely held soap.

He only nodded, took the soap pouch, and crossed his arms before stepping down from the grass to the sand and then into the water.

Asman hissed at the cold but waded deeper anyways, not stopping until the river water was lapping at his chest.

He slipped off his trousers and exhaled harshly as the cold enveloped his cock and balls. God, he had never enjoyed bathing in freezing rivers. Though, who had?

Luckily, the water soon became bearable and Asman set to work on dunking his head and scrubbing as much grime as he could with the soap.

As he was washing his face, he could see the dirt coming off in his hands, which made him grimace and scrub harder.

His back was the more difficult place to wash and Asman doubted he had gotten all the blood or dirt off. The soot came off easily with soap, but it did leave Asman feeling slightly bitter when he thought of where it came from.

Along with all his cleaning, he had begun to feel slightly better. He did not feel like he stunk, and even if he was cold it was a surprisingly nice change from the heat that this previous summer had been.

Asman usually loved summer, but this year had gotten well over the range that was comfortable; even Sam had said at some times it was unholy.

Now, Asman was clean of any dirt or sweat and he felt better about his appearance now that he could see just how much dirt was on his face.

Though there was still the issue of leaving the river. He still had no clothes on and definitely did not feel comfortable enough just to walk out of what little cover he had left with the water.

Dahlia was sitting off in the distance and sharpening a sword, so Asman thought if he got close enough he could call for her.

"Dahlia. Dahlia!" He first just spoke and then sharply yelled, but it seemed to get her attention well enough.

"Ah, sorry. Here; just change behind a tree I suppose." Dahlia shrugged and set a pile of clothes down onto the grass just before the short cliff.

Asman nodded and waiting for the woman to go back to cleaning her sword before he stalked forward quickly and snatched up the clothes, one hand covering his front for at least a bit of modesty.

He did not bother with moving away and towards a tree, but he did walk towards the patch of grass that was sloping down to meet the river so that his feet would not be covered in sand while he dressed.

The trousers and tunic provided were slightly bigger than his previous ones, but they did not smell like smoke and sweat and Asman was grateful. If he had to pull up the trousers more than often, it was a small price to pay.

The tunic was black and had long sleeves, while the trousers were a standard beige color. There were a pair of underwear also provided that Asman hesitantly slipped on, seeing as he did not know if these were someone else clothes or not and if so, it was a very personal thing to wear their undergarments.

Nonetheless, Asman did feel a lot more comfortable with clean and warm clothes on after he bathed.

When he returned to the camp, Dahlia stood back up with an unreadable look.

"Niallen wants you to see him." Dahlia winced slightly and did not meet Asman's gaze.

"Did he say why? You look nervous."

"No, he only said to tell you to come to his tent. He seemed strange is all." Dahlia shrugged slightly while crossing her arms.

"Alright. Thanks for telling me, Dahlia." Asman gave her a small smile if not for her comfort then for his.

Asman could only assume this was about what he said in the morning, though it could also be time that Niallen finally got sick of carrying him around and only decided to kill him.

Even though he could very well be walking to his death, Asman did so calmly and quickly. The other Guards all were looking at him as if they knew what their leader wanted, so he would not show them that he was actually very nervous.

"You wanted to see me, Niallen?"

Chapter Seven: Life

"Yes, come in, Asman."

Asman did just that and softly let out a breath, low enough that Niallen would not be able to hear it.

Niallen was sitting at his desk once more, this time only reading a parchment instead of writing on one.

When Asman stepped inside and closed the tent once more, Niallen set the paper down and looked up.

"I have decided that, with much thought, I would like to ask you to be a Blood Guard."

"What?" Asman furrowed his brows and looked at Niallen like he was insane.

"You said if you were not a prisoner then what were you. I am asking that you be a Guard instead of a prisoner." Niallen leaned forward and stared at Asman, who was standing and could physically feel the confusion wracking his brain.

"I cannot be a Blood Guard, Niallen. I do not even know how to hold a sword or fight. It would be a very poor decision to place me amongst the others out there."

Niallen only sighed lightly and stood, walking in front of the desk and crossing his arms.

"When choosing a new Blood Guard, it is my duty to look into the person and come to a decision. The Queen trusts my opinion on the matter, and she will trust me when I say that you are, so far, qualified for the Guard. All I ask is that you trust my decision as well." Niallen spoke with a steady tone and Asman felt as if he was being drafted for a war; in a way, he supposed he was.

The larger man was staring at him with certainty while Asman could only scoff.

"You are by far the most confusing and strangest men I have ever met. How does the Queen sleep at night knowing she appointed an idiot for a Guardsmen? You have only rarely shown traits of a good leader. Why would I join you when you do such stupid things like invite a scrawny damaged Feliasian to be in the Guard?"

Asman huffed in and out gently as he finished his rant. Immediately, he regretted what he said when Niallen stood and stalked over to him.

"I would mind your tongue. My Queen spent months trying to find the right person to do this job and I should hope she sleeps soundly seeing as she was correct. I have led this Guard for nearly a decade and will not let some boy try and criticize my leadership skills." Niallen growled out, his face coming close to Asman's. "The actions

I have carried out while you have been with us is only the result of me, despite your crude behavior, seeing that you have the possibility to become a great Guard. You are damaged, yes, but you have a fire in you that matches all the others out there."

Asman blanked while Niallen spoke, his face was flushed crimson as the mans face was mere inches away, his own eyes very easily dropping to the floor. He was speaking in a way that had Asman's heart thundering in his chest; not from attraction, but from the embarrassment of what Niallen was praising him for.

"You have not given me the chance to show you what a leader is, Asman. You judge me for mistakes that are only such in your mind. You need to acknowledge that your life will never be what it once was; that life ended the minute that Felias killed your brother." Niallen's voice softened only a little near the end.

Asman looked back up to Niallen's eyes the second that he mentioned his brother. His mouth was closed tight and his face scrunched.

"I will make sure that the Queen uses the information you give her well. If you wanted, you could live the rest of your days doing whatever you liked in Isadren; or you could join the Guard and guarantee that Felias is brought to justice for their crimes against your village and the others like it."

Niallen's eyes were filled with so much truth that Asman had trouble with focusing on anything else.

Niallen did not continue after that. He only went on to wait for what was likely Asman's response. But the man himself was still attempting to put his thoughts together.

No one had ever spoken to him like that. Even his brother was gentler with his words and rarely ever said such profound things. Asman's time with the merchant could not come close to how... important he felt after Niallen's words.

Asman of course had a small notion that what he was going to tell the Queen was important, but Niallen made it seem like Asman was so much more than his story, even if he did not feel as though all the time.

"It has been only three days. You believe you know me so well as to say all these things?" Asman spoke quietly, the only sound being those of the Guard members outside.

Niallen exhaled slowly and shook his head, the small hairs not pulled back gently swaying back and forth.

"No, but I know enough. I know what it feels like to have someone you care about killed, and how scary it can be to go without them." Niallen said just as quietly as Asman had been. "When we entered Stelai, I could tell you were angry. Why was that?"

Asman huffed gently and looked over to the side, focusing on where the sun was peaking through a hole in the canvas before averting his eyes back to Niallen.

"Nobody even cared, or knew, that a village only slighter smaller than their own had been destroyed and wiped out by the army. They likely will not know about the attack until someone bumps into the village, even then it will be months; who is to say that they will not be attacked by then?" Asman took a deep breath. "I wanted to tell everyone to run or leave or at least send their children away, but I also wanted to leave it be. Nobody would listen to me even if I did say something. They let themselves live in a country that is ruled by a King who would send an army to slaughter a whole village within his own land."

Niallen nodded in understanding, and a newer more determined look came across his face.

"Asman, this is what I was speaking off. Joining the Guard would give you the authority to help these people. We do not go to battle and fight in the war, we turn the tides of it. The Guard spends its days collecting information and carrying out smaller more important operations that therefore keep Felias from taking power over all of Calia. You could train and become one of us so that no more innocent people die."

Asman stared back at the man while thinking. He still could not wrap his head around why Niallen would ever want him to join his Guard.

He had successfully hit the man, but was a momentary underestimating lapse in judgement something to reward someone for?

"You really believe I could be a good Guard?"

"Yes."

Asman nodded softly and glanced down at the ground, the soft green grass was gently patted down from where he had been shifting his feet. They were barefooted still.

"If I were to agree to this, I would want to make some things understood." Asman said and looked back up to Niallen.

The man nodded for him to continue before stepping backwards some and crossing his arms. Asman felt a bit relieved that he had removed himself from Asman's personal space.

"I do not want magic used on any wounds without my knowledge. I still do not know much about Isadren and your culture so I would like to learn before I arrive there. If I should happen to climb a tree, I would prefer to be left alone for as long as possible." Asman listed easily after thinking for a moment.

"That is it?" Niallen questioned with a slightly furrowed brow, but shrugged. "I have no issue with these boons, but I would have imagined you to have more."

"What do you mean by that?" Asman frowned and made an offended noise.

"Only that there were others that had far more than you and with how you were treated I thought there were to be more problems had."

Asman flushed slightly and exhaled a short breath, crossing his own arms to mirror the mans.

"I do not have an issue with being treated harshly, only that no one does it with ill intent."

Niallen raised an eyebrow at that, but nodded once more anyway. He easily unraveled his arms and turned back to the desk, pulling from it a clean metal quill pen.

"The reason we are called the Blood Guard, is because I write our letters in my blood; and due to every member signing their name in

their blood when they join as so the queen knows who has joined."
Niallen explained and held out the pen for Asman to take. "Doing so
makes it so the queen can tell of someone's true intentions and their
emotions."

Asman gave the man a questioning glance, but took the pen either
way.

"How does she do that? I have heard that Isadrenians use magic
more often, is that the case here?" Asman asked and sighed shakily
before digging the pen into the meat of his palm, a fresh drop of
blood forming.

He hissed gently at the pain and dipped the tip of the quill back
into the blood, a small bead joining at the tips deep red in color.

"No, the Queen is a witch. She was born with Natural Magic, and
since blood is natural, she can use it to scry on someone." Niallen
explained while he watched Asman.

Niallen reached over to gently pull a paper so that it was in front
of Asman on the desk. There were words written as if it was a letter,
but it was in a language that Asman did not know.

"Isadrenians have a different language?"

"No, this is Ancient Calian. Not many know it due to how long
ago it was used. We use it to keep the contents of the letters safe if ever
we were ambushed." Niallen said lightly and pointed to the bottom
of the parchment. "Sign your name here and you will officially be a
Blood Guard. I must warn you there is magic involved, but hardly
enough to do anything. Only because you will be using your blood
with intent."

Asman inhaled deeply and nodded, but did not sign yet.

This was all going terribly fast, and even though Asman was all together ready to sign himself away. He could not help but wonder if this was the only choice.

At the moment, it seemed that was true. Asman did not want to remain a prisoner, even if he still did feel a bit of remorse for leaving. Though, what else would he do if he were not a prisoner? Joining the Guard seemed to be the easiest available route.

Niallen was the leader, and if he trusted that Asman would be a good member, what else could he do but say yes?

But what if Asman was not actually cut out for being a Guard? What if he became tired too easily or did not follow direction well? He certainly did not have the physical qualifications as of yet, but what if he did not have the right mental ones either?

"Asman. Do not overthink this. If we find you are not fit for this then you do not have to stay a Guard." Niallen spoke and paused Asman's thoughts as if he was inside the latters mind also.

Asman glanced over to the man and nodded once more. He felt that if he spoke he would retract his decision and then only annoy Niallen.

The blood on the pen had dried up already from how long Asman stood there, so it took him dipping the quill back into the growing spot of blood for it to be coated once more.

He pressed his lips together and with a fluid moment, scratched his name into the space on the paper with his blood.

The ruby liquid shined against the lantern light flickering on the desk. Asman watched as it soaked into the parchment and dried a fuller and deeper shade of red.

"Tomorrow we will begin training. Since we still have places to be, it will only be walking for the day. Do you think you can handle that?" Niallen spoke up, grabbing the pen from Asman's hand and walking behind the desk.

"Yes, I will be fine." Asman shook his head slightly; there was a strange feeling sitting low in his chest, almost like a stone had settled. "What is it that I am feeling?"

Niallen looked up with confused eyes and Asman frowned.

"You feel something?"

"Yes. Almost like a weight in my chest. Is that not supposed to happen?" Asman rubbed harshly at his ribs, the dull pain from the action only barely distracted him.

"Not exactly. Nothing should have happened since you do not have magic. Does it hurt any?" Niallen seemed to be wracking his brain before he opened a compartment in the desk and pulled forth another paper.

"No, just feels strange is all. Was it the magic?"

Niallen did not answer for a moment while he read the letter and Asman kept his breathing even. The weight was perfectly set between his lungs and felt as if he needed to cough.

When Niallen finally spoke it was only after he came from behind the desk and out towards the tent entrance, yelling for a Teran.

As time went on though, the weight got bigger and Asman finally began coughing, barely catching his breath between the fits. He was certain his face was red, and he could feel where spit had slicked his lips.

Behind him, the tent flap rustled open and the faded sound of talking broke through his coughing. Asman held a hand to his chest as his knees hit the grass. He had stopped coughing only so that he would not be taken unconscious by not breathing.

"Asman, focus on touching the grass. The green blades between your fingers and the way the roots reach into the earth." The new voice in the tent pointed out, a hand coming to rest on Asman's back.

He tried his best to follow the orders, but the weight in his chest only increased. A random person speaking to him only made him more confused.

The voice and Niallen argued for a moment. Asman's eyes fluttered shut while he gripped at the grass.

The hand on his back disappeared after a moment and Asman whimpered as he laid himself down in the grass on his back. He could feel the blades against his skull and ears, but it was dry now and without life. Perhaps there was a dead spot he had not noticed.

Niallen reacted to Asman falling with a yell of his name, though the mans ears had begun ringing a bit ago. Asman did not hear when Niallen and the voice left.

It was a strange feeling to not feel anything at all. It was as if he was numb while also being able to feel something else tugging at his mind and heart. The ground was cold and that was all he knew.

The weight was still there, but very slowly it started to ease. Asman very slowly could breath easier and the ringing in his ears quieted; the only sound was his own heartbeat and panicked yelling from outside the tent.

Somehow he knew that it was the Guard and that something bad had happened or was happening. It reminded Asman of Thamor's last day far too much for him to ignore the shouts of both urgency and consternation.

Even as the feelings in his arms and legs came back, it took a fair amount of time for Asman to be able to lift himself once more. The yelling from outside had quieted while he worked on inhaling and exhaling.

Asman finally opened his eyes and lifted his head once he felt the weight finally leave his chest. The numbness was replaced with frigid cold and fear.

He was alone in the tent, in the same spot he fell a period ago. The space was dark besides the lantern still barely lit on Niallen's desk.

The ground was the only thing different.

What was once green and plush grass beneath him was now dead and brown.

For as far as Asman could see within the tent, all the grass was dead; it crunched harshly as he pulled himself up from the lifeless ground.

Asman had done this. He knew he did. But the only question was how and why had this happened.

How could he have magic and not know about it?

Chapter Eight: Death

When he had walked outside of the tent, it was almost scary how barren it looked.

The fires were put out, yet every Guard members bags were still there. There were a couple pots of stew above the fire pits only they looked as if they had gone cold.

From where the horses had been tied, Asman found they were all gone and like inside the tent, the grass was brown and crisp.

The whole entirety of the small clearing near the river they had stopped in was empty and dead.

Asman could barely make out where a portion of light had broke through the trees. When he looked closer he noticed that it was the Guard along with the horses.

The sky was pitch black and the moon gone, so it took Asman a few stumbles to finally make his way within shouting distance of the Guard. That was when he heard Niallen clearly through the thicket.

"No! Asman, do not come any closer!" Niallen shouted, his words striking a sad chord in Asman. "Listen to me, Asman. Find the biggest and fullest tree you can and then touch it! Just hold on to it until we come to get you!"

Asman frowned, but nodded anyway, even if Niallen could not see him do so.

He stared up at the sky and squinted while he walked away, glancing at how big a tree was and how meany leaves it had. It took a moment for him to finally find one bigger than the rest.

Asman could barely see in front of himself, and without shoes it hurt to step on the fallen branches and dead grass beneath his feet. He felt horribly similar to the night he lost his brother.

The tears came unbidden, rolling down his cheeks without sound as he threw himself at the tree.

His face scrunched with sadness while his palms laid across the bark, the weight in his chest fully gone but hardly even noticed by Asman.

He waited for Niallen, or even Dahlia to come get him, but no one came. Asman was alone and crying while he stood confused against a tree.

When he realized no one was going to come, Asman slid down and curled up in the large roots at the base of the tree, one hand still resting there while his eyes closed.

The bark was rough against his fingertips, but it felt nice to have something to show that this was not a dream nor nightmare.

Would this change what Niallen had decided about his ability to be a Guardsman? Would he instead think Asman knew about this all along and was truly a spy for the Feliasian King? The man had accused him of it before, why would he not do so once more?

There was also the problem of how Asman had magic in the first place.

He had never once suspected that this was something to be cautious of. There were no signs pointing towards this, or instances that proved strange. The Fae Magic that healed his wound had not done anything, so then why had the apparent small amount from him signing himself as a Guard trigger something?

Asman was no fool. He was intelligent enough to know that it was him that did all that damage. There was no other option besides that; so why did he feel as if this is something to be afraid of?

More tears silently left his eyes while the bite of a cold night nipped at his toes. Would Niallen ever come, or was this the mans way of leaving him behind while the rest rode out to another spot?

It would be smart of them to do so. What with Asman killing the surrounding areas flora and almost its fauna. He would never forgive himself if Berry or any other horses died from a lack of control on this magic. It would be even worse if any of the Blood Guards were killed either.

"Over the hillI will be waiting on for youI won't pretendThat you don't mean nothing to meCome now, come nowCome back now, come back now."

Asman sniffed quietly as he lowly sang out the words of a song; the same song that he had heard two bards sing now.

"The doubt will creepAnd crawl in on youThe dark can leapAnd fall upon youCome back now, come back now."

The rest of the short song was hummed, seeing as Asman did not remember all of the words and he was beginning to feel a tad too tired to continue.

He had shut his eyes a short moment ago, and his breathes were coming in short puffs even if he had been crying. If he could see himself he was sure he would look pathetic.

Even so, Asman sighed gently and adjusted once more to get more comfortable; as much as he could against a tree trunk. The cold night barely kept him awake even though it would have had him shivering painfully before this.

He had napped earlier in the day, but there seemed to be a bone deep tiredness washing over him as he kept his hand to the tree. Asman assumed it had something to do with the magic, but ignored thinking any more about the subject. Instead, he let himself drift away.

With the crickets chirping safely, and the sound of the Guards far off in the distance, Asman felt the first leaf fall as he fell asleep.

"Asman. It is time to wake, Asman."

Said man hummed and opened his eyes, peeking over to see Dahlia and Niallen next to him. Niallen was crouched and had a hand resting on Asman's shoulder, gently squeezing to wake him.

It was bright outside, with the birds chirping and cicadas singing from the forest canopy.

Asman had a blanket on him, but the sun was shining now and he was a bit warm. He could not remember receiving the blanket.

"We are sorry it took so long to see you. We had to make sure it was safe before getting too close." Dahlia frowned slightly and gave Asman an apologetic look.

He nodded and blinked as he sat up, the blanket falling off his shoulder and onto his lap.

"How do you feel?" Niallen asked simply. "What happened last night was a bit of a surprise to us and it seems you too."

"I am... confused, I suppose." Asman exhaled softly, briefly looking around before frowning.

The ground was covered in dead leaves; strange for it still being summer. When he looked up, he found that the tree he had been resting against was barren, though still alive. He was almost certain he had stumbled into a full one last night.

"That is fine. It is alright to be confused, especially since Niallen and I are the same." Dahlia pinched her face. "You never knew you had magic?"

Asman reached up to rub at his eyes, running a hand through his hair absently while skating his head.

"No. No, I never... never even suspected as such." Asman frowned; if he knew he had magic only a few days earlier perhaps he could have saved Sam.

How could he not know that he had magic? Was it normal to not know something so important about yourself for so long?

"Death Magic is a fickle thing. Those who have it often are killed before they grow into it, those who survive usually end up dying either way. It is not something you should like to have; the forces that are at play with your kind often break its users." Niallen stated in a hard tone, the words only making Asman more and more upset.

"Break in what way?" Asman huffed out, a fearful look on his face.

"There is a lot more to Death Magic than just being able to kill things. I would prefer to wait until we reach Isadren to properly tell you, as the queen might be better at explaining than I would be." Niallen frowned and looked off to side, staring at the leaves covering the ground.

Asman exhaled sharply and glared at Niallen, but did not say anything more.

He only picked up the blanket off his lap and began lifting himself off the ground. Though, he slightly wavered when his mind fuzzed a little at the action.

"You used a lot of magic last night. I would prefer for you to take it easy , you do not need to walk today and you should keep plenty of fluids in your body. It is still early enough that there should be stew left." Niallen stood up straight also, coming to hover over Asman carefully.

"Am I a Guard, Niallen?" Asman asked and kept his gaze straight at the man.

"Even though there was difficulties with the magic, you still signed your name. So, yes, you are a Blood Guard as of last night." Niallen nodded.

"Then I will walk today. I feel fine besides the dizziness, but that will go away as soon as I eat and drink." Asman stated shortly, "I will not give up on doing this just because new things have come to light; you wanted me to be a Guard, so I will be."

Niallen stared back at Asman with an unidentifiable look, but the latter only nodded and glanced at Dahlia before walking away.

Asman watched him go with a twinge of annoyance. Niallen was one of the only men who could make him feel like he lost when he had in fact won the conversation.

"Are you sure you should walk today? We do not know the weather that could happen, and the only break you would get would be near noon. I would hate for a repeat of-"

"Dahlia, I will be fine. My head is already clearing as we speak. I have been on my feet longer than a day at times, I am sure I can keep up for the time we ride." Asman smiled softly at the woman, already feeling better that she would be kinder than Niallen.

"I only hope that you do not push yourself further than need be. I have seen strong men and women fall from thinking they could handle some of the things they cannot." Dahlia sighed gently, turning and nodding for Asman to begin walking.

The crunching of leaves was pleasing to Asman in a way, though the dead foliage only lasted for so long before instead of the crunching of leaves it was the soft cracking of dry grass.

Now that the sun was up, Asman could see just how far the death had spread.

The clearing that they had settled in was a fair bit from the road, but you could see it through the trees. Asman could barely see that the decay had spread to just beyond the road. On their side of the river, there were trees overhanging and letting go leaves every moment; they were not as bad as the one Asman had slept against.

A positive note was that Asman could not see anything on the other side of the river, so at least the water stopped his uncontrolled magic for him.

Last night, it had felt like Asman had walked far away from the camp; after Niallen had yelled for him to find a tree, he felt as if he stumbled and tripped along for forever till he finally found the right one. Though, now that he was walking back to the camp, he could see that he actually did not go all to far away.

The tree was within the limits of the dead grass, but on the outer edges. Niallen's tent was the center of a large circle of death.

Once Asman and Dahlia actually stepped inside the area filled with fire pits and packed bags, Asman could see just how bad the grass had been killed.

Reaching out from Niallen's tent was a even darker and more charred circle of grass, as if the plants were rotting from the root up.

Asman felt terrible that he had done this to the clearing, seeing as it would not likely recover for more than five years. Once it was dead there was no coming back.

Along with the pitiful grass, there was also the way that the rest of the Guards looked at him.

Most of them looked at him with a side of caution, drawing back their shoulders as if readying to fight. Asman tried not to make eye contact, but when he did, he quickly looked away and to show enough submission that they would leave him be.

The rest of the Guard seemed almost inquiring or wondering. They did not seem scared, but watched him carefully with prying eyes that begged for an answer to what Asman had done.

Regardless of the stares, Asman held his head high as Dahlia led him to one of the fires with a stew pot hanging over it.

There were a few men and a couple women standing there also, but Dahlia ignored them as she reached for a clean bowl to ladle stew into.

"So, you did this to the grass then?" One of the men piped up eventually.

Asman glanced to him and inhaled sharply, hoping that this man did not think of him as a threat.

"Yes. I was unaware that I have magic, so when I signed my name there was an adverse reaction." Asman said and took the bowl from Dahlias hand when offered.

"Some fucking reaction. Even Teran's little discovery did not kill a whole clearing." The man snorted and jutted a thumb out at the man next to him.

Asman glanced over to Teran and felt the memories click into place from last night.

"You were the one that tried to help me last night." Asman stated, "I should thank you for doing so, even if I did not listen all that well."

Teran waved a hand dismissively and smiled.

"It was a shot in the dark, Niallen calling for me to help. I am the only Guard who has gone through something similar to you in terms of magic. I do not believe I could have help you any even if you did listen. My magic is different from yours, so I would have had no clue how to deal with yours."

"Still, thank you." Asman stirred lazily at the stew in his hands with a spoon. "What type of magic do you have?"

"Just a type of Water Magic. It stays dormant most of the time, but signing my name reacted because of the Blood Magic used. I am afraid my becoming was more of a small rainstorm than a culling of the areas wildlife." Teran chuckled easily, but Asman's heart twinged painfully at how unimportant he made it seem.

"Hey, it was still impressive. You drenched all the Guards and made us all pile into Niallen's tent for the night." One of the women spoke up with a sharp laugh. "I would say that annoying Niallen is a win for all of us; he gets funny when he tries to be mad at us."

"Pilla, that is only because he feels bad making fun of your ugly mug when you cannot help that you look like a dogs arse." The man from before teased and made Pilla expell an affronted noise.

Asman watched amused as Pilla tackled the man to the ground, the two wrestling while Teran laughed heartily.

He continued to watch while he ate the stew, the pressure in his head from before nearly all gone as he drank down the rest of the broth.

So far, Asman felt like perhaps his magic was not as big of a deal as Niallen made it out to be.

No, right now, Asman felt as if he had finally found somewhere that he was accepted despite his past or flaws.

Chapter Nine: Water

With the sun still low in the sky, and Asman's belly full of stew and water, the Guard set out for the fifth day of Asman being with them.

Dahlia had made sure to give Asman a water canteen so that he was hydrated throughout the day, and even though he would likely be fine just drinking at noon, he still was grateful that she thought of him.

She sometimes reminded Asman of the second girl he had once bedded. Though, he could without pause say that he had no sort of sexual feelings for Dahlia.

Her hair was dark and almost always pulled back in a braided bun. She was tan and had deep brown eyes that reminded Asman of the soil right after a rain. Asman especially liked how Dahlia smelled like the forest and the ground that matched her eyes.

When he had met Cheden, the man that had wrestled Pilla that morning, Asman was almost sure the two had to be related somehow.

Chedens own hair was braided, though he kept it down and let the small and intricate braids sit handsomely against the deep brown locks.

Though, when Asman asked, Dahlia only laughed and said that they were not related and only from the same area.

The Silvania Desert was almost as far south as you could go within the continent of Calia. Asman had heard of it, but had never exactly wished to go as he did not prefer to melt out of his skin.

There were a good amount of Guards from there, including the man that had thrown Asman over his shoulder while they were in Stelai. His name was Stulvon and although he came from the same place as Dhalia and Cheden, his skin was much darker than theirs.

Along with Stulvon, there was a woman called Malkin that came from Silvania. Both her and Stulvon had dark skin and hair that was strung together in thick ropes; there were small rings throughout that glistened in the sun.

Not only were there Guards from Silvania, there were also Guards from Sedrey, Isadrens southern and Felias' northern neighbor. The kingdom had always been neutral during the war, but there were rumors that some had joined the Isadrenian army in secret. Asman had never believed it before.

Those from Sedrey were Pilla, a man named Malon, a man named Hutch, and Jacksill, who Asman knew from when Niallen had called for him to pay the stable master in Stelai.

There were also those from the Galdrin Islands, just off the coast of Silvania. The Islands were known for being beautiful and exotic, though it was still as hot as Silvania, only with less sand and more moist forests.

Asman had not met any of the Galdrins that were in the Guard, but Dahlia had still told him their names while they walked.

Finnet and Vanora were sister and brother, and Rhinn was the other Galdrin. There were not many as Guards, but they still were close with everyone else despite not being with their people.

The other Guard members were all Isadrenians, including; Niallen, Teran, Hilcren, Strena, Elsten, Larrel, Nyana, Danyel, Aelina, Seraphina, Brandla, Hamen, and Marrion.

Asman felt overwhelmed by the influx of information that Dahlia had told him, but as she pointed them all out, it was easier to remember who was who.

He was sure that he would still forget everyone's names at times, but it still felt nice to know he was at all trusted with that knowledge.

Dahlia spoke to him for most of the day, and even Teran and Pilla joined in as the day passed by. The conversation was a pleasant distraction from all the walking that Asman was participating in.

The sun was almost perfectly overhead when they finally stopped for a moment; mostly only because of the horses need for water, but Asman was sure that the Guards needed a bit of time to stretch. For him though, it was a time to sit and take a breath.

The source of water they came upon was a small creek, likely a branch off of the river from the previous night.

Asman, even though he was accustomed to walking, was still out of breath from moving the large distance they had covered.

He took to standing against a tree as he rested, not wanting to sit and then dread having to stand again.

The horses drank and grazed some, and Asman did the same though his water was from the canteen and he ate only some dried fish. The food did not taste as well as what the meat had, but Asman still took it from Teran gratefully.

"How are you faring, Asman?"

Said man looked over to where Niallen had walked up to him with his own dried fish in hand, teeth working at tiny bones as he spoke.

Asman swallowed his mouthful of water and nodded slightly, the taste of the sea still sitting oddly in his mouth.

"Well enough. Hot, if anything." Asman shrugged; he would never tell Niallen that he was actually tired from walking so much.

"Your head is clear? No dizziness or pain?" Niallen asked with a careful eye.

"No. Not since this morning; the water and food has helped."

Asman felt as if he was being interrogated by his brother after he would have an episode and his in a tree for too long.

"Good; and the boots? I hope Cheden was able to find some that fit comfortably?"

"Yes, yes, they are comfortable."

Niallen nodded and bit into another small fish, the dried skin cracking loudly even over the sound of the rest of the Guard. Asman watched vaguely disgusted while the man chewed through the fish and swallowed.

"I think we will trot until Lake Dewain. It is only a short distance from here but there is a village on the edge that we will stay in tonight. Are you up to that?" Niallen nodded his head over to where the road went on before shoving the rest of the fish in his mouth.

"I will be fine." Asman stated shortly, peering down at the last fish in his hand before grimacing and holding it out for Niallen.

Niallen smirked and gently swatted at Asman's hand.

"Eat it. If only to keep your belly full." He said before walking away back towards Stulvon.

Asman frowned and looked back down to the fish, sticking his tongue out and shuddering before he shut his eyes and stuffed the small piece down his throat, barely chewing before swallowing and gulping down water.

He absolutely did not like the way the bones crunched and snapped, or the way that he could see the fishes eyes staring at him unblinkingly.

While the rest of the Guard waited for the horses, Asman made sure to refill the canteen with the creek water and of course say hello to Berry.

She was standing next to another horse, a gelding that was similar in color to her own coat, so Asman was a bit hesitant to walk up to her in fear that the other horse would kick him for getting to close.

Though, it seemed that the horse actually did not care that much and only swished his tail back and forth to rid the flies off his back.

Berry was eating, but did not seemed to disturbed by Asman's presence either, so he easily fell into running his hands through her mane.

Asman smiled softly when she picked up her head and lipped at his shoulder before going back to the grass. He hummed a happier tune and went forth on braiding a tiny bit in her mane.

When he finished with the braid, he went on to another one, and then one after that, and soon there were six small braids hanging from her mane.

He figured he had best not out too many, as Niallen would probably take them out anyway, but just in case, Asman tied them off with blades of grass.

As he saw the Guards return to their horses, he quickly made it seem as if he was only tightening the straps on the tack before walking off back to the road.

Asman waited patiently for the Guard to start off on the path again.

When they did, it was not for another few moments that Niallen made the move to start trotting instead of walking.

The rest of the Guard followed easily, spurring on their horses to follow Berrys lead. Asman followed too, jogging to stay next to Dahlias horse, as she and her gelding were the last in the group so that Dahlia could speak to Asman.

Asman kept up easily, though he was still hot and worried that if he kept his shirt on it would be drenched in sweat. So, with a swift move he pulled the long sleeved tunic off and traded it off to Dahlia, who had held out a hand for the shirt when she saw what was happening.

The cool air felt much better against Asman's skin rather than the tunic that, even though it was thin, was no match for the high noon sun.

It felt a tad uncomfortable without his shirt on, but luckily he and Dahlia were the only ones to see. Asman did not mind if Dahlia saw, as he was sure she would not care if he did not have the same amount of defined muscles as the other men.

They stayed at the same pace all before Asman could spot the lake through the trees and smoke over the horizon. That was when Niallen called him to the front to jog next to Berry instead.

Asman frowned but did so anyway. The rest of the Guard had spilt through the middle so that he could have a clear path to the leader.

Without word, Niallen kicked Berry into a medium speed gallop. Asman groaned and ran off after the man, seeing that up ahead was the village that he had spoke of.

He could not tell how fast they were going, but Asman inhaled and exhaled rapidly while he pushed his legs to carry him further and catch up to Niallen, who was only a small distance away.

When he finally caught up and was running beside Berry, Asman smiled mentally and went even faster than before, sprinting so that he was going in front of Niallen and quickly gaining ground as the village got closer and closer.

He could hear the hoofbeats behind him, but it only pushed him to go faster.

Asman furrowed his brows as he felt the strain in his legs become even more prominent than before. His throat was dry and his hair was sticking to his forehead from where the sweat had matted it down, but he desperately wanted to beat Niallen in a race.

The village was even closer now, close enough that Asman could see where a street vendor was selling apples.

He could still hear Berry behind him, but she was quieter now. Perhaps only because his blood was pounding in his ears.

In the back of his mind he knew he had to stop, but what he actually did was keep going until a man walked in front of his path and Asman slid to a stop instead.

Because he stopped so suddenly, his feet continued to move on the gravel and in a moment his arse hit the ground with a puff of dust.

"Ow." Asman muttered and stayed in the dirt for a moment while catching his breath.

"Are you alright?"

Asman looked up to see the man that he had almost ran into holding out a hand.

"Y-yes, I was just... racing a horse." Asman stuttered and nearly choked on the greedy breaths he was still taking.

The man was gorgeous.

His hair was blond and curly, with bright blue eyes that reminded Asman of the lake they were near. His smile was stunning, all full of straight white teeth. He was taller than Asman and his hands were huge, so when the latter took one he could have fainted.

"Well, it seems you won at least. My name is Wentt." The man continued to hold a hand as he smiled.

Asman flushed and took the hand, barely using the other man to lift himself but keeping his hand because it felt nice.

"Thank you, Wentt. My name is Asman, it is a pleasure to meet you." Asman smiled softly.

"Oh, the pleasure is mine. It is not everyday that a shirtless man almost runs me over. Especially not one as beautiful as you." Wentt chuckled lightly as he flipped over Asman's hand and raised it to his lips, kissing softly at the knuckles there.

Asman blushed hotly and giggled, he was still out of breath from the run and having an attractive male compliment him did nothing to help.

"Are you staying here for long? I would love to show you the lake, there is a-"

"Asman!"

He snapped his head around to see Niallen approaching, he had slowed down to a walk so when he made for Berry to stop it was more smooth than Asman's.

Asman quickly drew his hand from Wentts, crossing his arms over his bare chest and hoping that the flush on his cheeks was not too noticeable.

"Niallen." Asman greeted and pointedly ignored the way that said man was staring at Wentt.

"Come, the rest will be here shortly so that gives us time to find the Inn." Niallen said shortly and dismounted Berry with a quick move.

"Oh, I could help if you wanted? I know exactly where the inn and the stables are." Wentt chimed in and Asman froze, still looking at Niallen to see what the man would do.

He seemed to think on it for a moment before nodding once. Asman relaxed slightly at the movement.

"Great, just follow me then." Wentt smiled widely and reached over to place a hand onto the small of Asman's back.

Asman exhaled sharply and honed in on the warm hand against his bare skin. It had been almost a year since he had been touched like this by another man that was not his brother. Of course, he did not have the same feelings for Sam as he did for Wentt or the merchant.

He quietly let the man guide him down the street, his head down except for the glances he would give Niallen occasionally.

Niallen would meet his gaze almost every time with different expressions, his eyes were wary but also slightly annoyed while also holding something back; it was almost as if he wanted to say something but could not.

"Here we are." Wentt finally stated as they walked up to what was clearly a stable. "I do not know how many more are coming, but there are likely fifteen open stalls."

Asman felt as the hand against his back moved so that Wentts knuckles were casually making circles against his skin and he shuddered.

Niallen made a humming noise beside him and walked off before Asman could even look at him, Berry sticking next to him as they went off into the stable and left Asman alone with Wentt.

"He is certainly a character." Wentt spoke quietly as soon as the man was out of sight. "Is he the one you were racing?"

Asman inhaled slowly and nodded, letting his arms fall to his side as he felt himself simmer a bit more.

"You tense around him. You are not in any danger, are you?" Wentt questioned, his hand traveling against the span of Asman's back with purpose.

"No, of course not. He only... he makes me nervous sometimes is all. We have only known each other for a few days, so I have yet to figure him out." Asman furrowed his brows, but relaxed them when Wentt gently scraped his nails across his shoulder blades.

"Well, perhaps once you have spent more time with him the feeling with pass." Wentt shrugged once, "I suppose I should leave you be so that you can settle, the Inn is just there so you should have no trouble finding it. If you ever feel the need though, my home is just two doors down from the inn to the left. Come see me if you want, but no harm done if not."

Wentt drew his hand back and stepped in front of Asman, picking up his hand once again in order to place another kiss there at the knuckles.

"Hope to see you soon, Asman."

Asman smiled and nodded, watching as Wentt turned his back to him and started off down the road towards the inn.

Niallen would not mind if Asman spent one night away from the Guard, would he?

Chapter Ten: Sound

Asman woke in the morning to his legs and back achingly sore.

As it figured, all it took was Asman rooming with Dahlia and asking for her to keep a secret for him to sneak away.

Wentt was happy to allow him to stay, and even happier that Asman was all too eager to have a night filled with pleasure.

He was a careful and kind lover, and although Asman was left feeling satisfied, he also wished that the man would have been a tad rougher.

Either way, Asman had woken up with his lower back twinging in pain and his legs sore from the walk the day before.

Wentts bed was comfortable, but Asman was sure to get up as soon as he woke for fear that the Guard and Niallen would see he was missing.

Luckily, the sun had just begun to rise into Wentts windows, shining golden light over were the man himself was sleeping soundly in the nude. Asman sighed at the sight before going around to collect his clothes which had been thrown off during the night.

Silently, Asman used a slip of parchment and ink pen on Wentts desk to write a short letter stating he was leaving. He hoped the man would not be hurt by it, but at the same time, Asman absolutely needed to leave as quickly as possible.

He found his boots near the door, and snatched them up before quietly exiting the home, wincing at the clang of the lock latching.

The Inn was indeed only a couple doors down, so it was a quick walk as Asman rushed to get back to him and Dahlias room.

When he opened the door to the Inn, he was pleased to find that nobody was there in the main room. Only the Innkeeper, who glanced at him with a knowing look and went back to her menial task of sorting papers.

Asman sighed internally and went forth to go upstairs, his bare feet occasionally making the floorboards creak. He winced every time the wood sounded its displeasure, but eventually got up the stairs.

"Asman? What are you doing awake?"

He froze as he turned the corner, Niallen standing there as he shut the door to his own room.

"I had to, uh, take a piss." Asman gestured with his boots to the stairs, his heart picking up slightly at the lie.

"Why are your boots off?" Niallen raised an eyebrow and stepped closer. His bag was slung over his shoulder and his sword dangling off his hip.

"I-I did not want to wake anyone."

"Really? Because to me, it smells as if that was a lie. It smells as if you spent the night somewhere else, had a bath, and partook in some very intimate activities," Niallen's look hardened as he leaned forward and inhaled sharply. "With that man from earlier it seems."

Asman blushed and took a step back, glancing off to the side with embarrassment.

"You should not be able to smell that." Asman scoffed and crossed his arms, still not meeting Niallen's gaze.

"But I do, and I should not have to be the one to tell you that fucking people you have just met is a bad idea. Especially not when you are needed for a much larger purpose and it is crucial that you stay alive."

Asman bristled harshly and snapped his eyes up to meet Niallen's, anger fuzzing his mind.

"I can fuck whoever I want, Niallen. I am grown enough to know when it is dangerous or not. It is not as if I was spilling every secret I own, in fact, there was little to no talking at all. There was no harm done to either the Guard or me, so do not act as if you are worried for my wellbeing when all you are worried about is whether or not I am alive enough to tell my story." Asman ranted, his face flushed in anger rather than humility now.

He did not wait for Niallen to respond before shoving past him and walking off towards Dahlias room.

When he reached the door, he roughly turned the handle and flung open the door. Seeing that Dahlia was awake and gathering her bag, Asman slammed the door behind him and shoved himself into the wooden chair next to the door, throwing his boots off to the side.

"Well, I sure hope everyone was awake by now. If not, they are now."
Dahlia piped up after a moment.

Asman ran a hand through his hair, inhaling and exhaling quickly
as he held back tears. He hated feeling ashamed by something he
should not at all feel ashamed by. He hated the constant arguing with
that bullheaded man.

He was an adult, and should be able to choose who he is bedded by.
It was hard enough having to sneak away from Sam and hide himself
from the village while the merchant or bards were there.

Niallen made it seem as if what he did was dirty and wrong. Asman
had been under the impression that the man would not care about
his interest in men, seeing as Dahlia had said as such when he had
spoke to her last night. Not only did Niallen judge him for his choice
of lover, but he had also brought up the true reason he was there also.

Although Niallen had made it seem as such at first, Asman was not
a Guard because they wanted him to be, he was a Guard because it
made sure he thought he had a place just enough that Niallen would
not have to make him a prisoner again.

Perhaps is was Asman's fault to think he had enough freedom to
have sex. Perhaps he was in a situation where he only had the amount
of privilege that Niallen deemed fit.

"Asman? You okay?" Dahlia asked as she stepped forward towards
him.

Asman nodded and inhaled sharply, standing to collect the boots
he had thrown before sitting back down on one of the beds.

He silently pulled the black shoes on, tying the laces with a certain amount of hostility.

"Alright. Did you at least have a good night?" Dahlia moved to retrieve her sword from the bed.

"Yes. He was a perfect gentleman at the least." Asman huffed gently. "Unlike some men are."

"Men are usually like that; that is why I choose not to fuck them." Dahlia chuckled lightly while tossing her hair over her shoulder.

Asman smiled and finished tying the last bow on his boots. He watched as Dahlia struggled to pull her hair into a bun, the braid gone from sleeping.

"I could help if you want? I know how to plait hair." Asman offered easily. As a boy, his best friend was a girl, who also turned into his first lover. She had asked him to do her hair sometimes, so Asman asked her mother to teach him.

In the end, he mastered the art of plaiting hair and all of the girls friends were asking for him to do it for them. Asman, looking back, can see that was probably a flirtation that he gave into.

"Oh, yes, that sounds wonderful. I would do my hair but it is way too early for me to do anything that will look good." Dahlia sighed and sat down next to Asman, a yawn stretching her mouth open.

Asman chuckled and stifled his own yawn, adjusting along with Dahlia so that he was at her back and her head was tipped back.

He ran his fingers through her hair to get the knots before sectioning off the hair.

It took a few moments, but in the end there was a slightly loose plait running from her head to just below her shoulder blades.

"Thank you, Asman. It looks great." Dahlia smiled as she gently ran a hand over the braid while looking in the mirror. "We should probably go and meet the others now. The other horses have been outside all night so we need to check on them."

Asman exhaled slowly and nodded, following the woman when she grabbed her bag up and stepped out into the hall.

It seemed that there were only a few Guards still not present when the two made there way out to the stables. Hutch, Seraphina, and Hamen had all went to purchase more food seeing as there were twenty five people all together and that many people ate a decent amount.

Asman made it a point to ignore Niallen, who was sending looks to where Asman was talking with Teran and Dahlia.

Both seemed to notice his deliberate ignorance but did not say anything, and when the last three Guards came to join them, Teran laughed and offered for Asman to ride on his horse with him.

Asman politely declined, hoping that if he walked it would cancel any reason for Niallen to speak to him. The road the day before had been tiring, though not so much that Asman could not do it again. Of course, he was still sore from that walk and the activities from the night, but anything was better than having Niallen continue to berate him for little things.

With everyone back onto their horses and the sun glittering across the lake, the Guard made their way off onto the path once more.

The day had started off nice in the morning, but as it went by, the clouds became thicker and sun hid behind them. It was luckily not dark enough to prove storms as of yet, but Asman had a feeling that the coming night would have a worse chance of raining if the clouds did not dissipate.

He did not know the Guards procedure for rain, or if they planned to stop at another village tonight, but Asman hoped that they would not have to sleep in the rain.

Even if the weather was unknown for the future, at the moment it felt nice and cool.

Asman usually did not like the cold, but seeing as the day before had been remarkably warm while he wore a long sleeved tunic, the change of pace was welcomed as he walked.

It was just after their break near the middle of the day that the weather finally showed its hand.

Thunder rumbled off in the distance, and Asman could see where the dark clouds were moving quickly towards them. The scent of rain was thick in the air, and with no sign of a village being close by, Asman frowned at the thought of what they would do.

Niallen did the smart thing and pulled them off to the side, claiming a small break in the trees as where they would settle.

There was enough shelter for the horses to stand beneath the trees, but there was only enough room for likely Niallen's tent and a fire or two.

A pond nearby was large enough for the horses to drink from, but small enough that the Guard could not do so at risk of catching a stomach bug. Asman figured if it came to it, the rainwater could be caught and drank.

He watched silently as Niallen and a few of the others set up the tent, though this time they added a second wing that added to the structure nearly half the length as usual.

Niallen's tent was not normally something you could fit twenty five people into, in fact, Asman would be surprised if it held more then five comfortably. But with the addition it would the Guard enough room to at least lay out shoulder to shoulder.

The rest of the Guard filed in easily and without hassle, but Asman was left frowning and staring at the tent with disdain.

All the times he had been in that tent were times he could very happily do with forgetting, and Asman could tell that at some point during the night, Niallen would try and talk to him.

Dahlia was fortunately still by her horse, so at least he would not be the last one or alone when he entered. The rain was still fast approaching, the leaves of the canopy shaking with the wind.

The Guards had at least had the mind to stake down the tent and tie off various corners on the nearby trees so that it would not collapse during the storm.

"Are you coming?" Dahlia sounded from beside him, her horses tack in her arms and her bag over her shoulder.

Asman exhaled lightly and nodded, following her as she walked over to the tent and entered. Everyone had mostly settled when Asman came inside the tent.

Niallen was sitting on his own bedroll and speaking with Stul-von, both of them with a few dried fish in their hands and chewing mouths.

Asman moved on quickly and continued to look around while Dahlia led them to where they would be settling for the night.

Most everyone was either eating or talking, or situating their things so that everyone would be comfortable.

Dahlia unfortunately could only lead them to the first available spot, which was to the left of the door; seeing as Niallen was to the right of the door, Asman was not particularly happy with this claim.

Though, at least Dahlia took the spot closest to Niallen so that Asman was sandwiched between her and Cheden, who had handed him a few strips of, thankfully, dried meat.

Asman stayed sitting up while he ate, but Dahlia laid down as soon as she settled along with most of the Guard. Cheden sat next to him for a bit, though he ended up lying down also.

He knew that it would probably be best for him to sleep also, but his mind would not let him do so.

The sounds of the night were irritating him.

The frogs and owls and bugs hidden in the grass. The rain that had started to pitter against the roof of the tent; it all felt too alive.

Asman had already been on edge from his argument with Niallen, now he felt anxious from both the feeling that the man was watching him and the faint whispering that had started up.

All his muscles had stiffened when the voices began to sing haunt-ingly into his ears. Asman could not help when his hands came up to clap over his ears, hoping that if he could not hear all the noises of life then the whispering would stop.

With no such luck, his eyes flitted around the tent, seeing that nobody was even paying attention to him; except for Niallen, who had halted his conversation with Stulvon in order to watch Asman.

Asman's breathing picked up when the voices got louder, making him quietly whimper and stand. He ignored Dahlia and Niallen's look of concern in favor of bolting out into the rain.

The rain drops pelted him as he ran through the cold wet night, dodging trees while he desperately tried to shut out the sounds.

He did not stop until almost ran into a larger oak tree, the bark grabbing at his tunic as if reaching to keep him there.

Asman did as it asked and pressed his forehead against the tree, the voices continuing to climb in volume until they were almost screaming at him.

They told him to kill the tree. To snuff out the light that was its life just as he had done before. Asman was grateful that they had switched to the tree instead of begging him to kill the Guard, to kill Niallen and Dahlia and Cheden until their lights were gone too.

The weight in his chest was back also, almost as bad as it was when he had signed his name.

Asman was confused as to why this was happening now; why not during the day or yesterday?

"Stop, please. Please stop, no, I do not want to, no." Asman muttered and clenched his eyes shut tightly.

He did not want to kill another tree and allow himself to be roped into a life where he had to desecrate living things in order to feel sane.

The voices hissed in anger, the words they had been speaking merging into yells and screaming. Asman sobbed as the sounds brought him back to that night, with the people he had grown up with wailing while they were massacred.

"Stop. Stop. Stop. Shut up, shut up, shut up." Asman cried, the water from the rain and tears from his eyes mixing against his cheeks.

He let go of his ears, the defense had done nothing against the voices. Asman wept loudly and lifted his head off the tree, bring his palms down in desperation. He wanted it to stop, the voices and the weight and the helpless feeling.

The bark was rough beneath his hands while Asman focused on what he had felt the night before last. He did not want to kill the tree, but he had to. The voices were yelling in his mind and fogging all that he could ever think of.

"Sorry. I am sorry, please I do not want to, I am sorry." He whimpered to the tree.

Asman could feel a thrumming beneath his palms, the old oak having almost a tangible heartbeat; it only made Asman feel worse.

It was only a tree, but it was still alive and had a purpose for living just the same as any human. The tree from the other night had only lost its leaves, but Asman was sure that this one would not survive.

The tears still fell quickly down his face as he finally felt the dam collapse. All that was holding him back broke and tore through him into the tree.

Asman wailed throughout it all, his hands shaking even as they sat steady on a dying tree. He could not control himself while he dragged the life from this creature; as he snuffed out the light.

The rain was still coming down heavily, with thunder groaning every so often, but all Asman could hear was the creaking from the tree as the wood shifted and died.

When his hands had nothing to rest on he finally opened his eyes and took a step back.

There was no tree left anymore, only a decaying stump that was blackened by the ash of its previous body.

Asman exhaled shakily and held the back of his hand to his mouth, feeling as if he would be sick while he felt the after effects of what he had done.

Though, he did not get a chance to do so due to the way his body fell of its own accord, his mind failing to keep itself awake while his back and head hit the ground with a thud.

All he felt before darkness was the gentle drops of rain splashing onto his face.

Chapter Eleven: Touch

Asman woke the next morning warm, his body covered in furs and blankets.

He hummed at the feeling of them against his bare chest and opened his eyes slowly while he continued to wake, a smooth grey light of day making his eyes sensitive.

He was in Niallen's tent, with nearly the whole Guard looking at him with both concern and tension. It startled him at first, but as the events of the previous night filtered into his mind he froze.

"Oh. Oh, god." Asman whimpered and felt his heart prickle with panic.

Did they know? Did the Guard know that he destroyed a tree? That he could not control himself and so he had burned a living creature to just a stump so that voices would stop screaming at him?

Tears formed at his lower lash line and his breathing picked up as he sat up and tore the furs and blankets off of him. He was not wearing the same trousers as he had last night, but at least these were dry. Asman was only skeptical at who had stripped and dressed him.

He shook those thoughts away easily while he pushed to try and stand up. Asman had almost succeeded, but was intercepted by Niallen's arm coming out to discourage him getting up.

"Stop. You need to rest after what-"

"D-do not touch me. Please, please do not touch me I can not control it, Niallen." Asman scooted as far back as he could into the tent wall and way from Niallen's arm.

"Asman, you should calm down. You do not need to control it, your magic is depleted from what you achieved last night. It will likely be days until you are able to do any damage." Niallen spoke gently and raised a hand non threateningly.

Asman only raised a hand to his hair and shook his head, clenching his eyes shut and gritting his teeth while he forced the tears to disappear.

"Achieved? Achieved... to kill a creature that meant no harm. Achieved giving in to voices screaming at me to murder like I had choice in the matter." Asman's brows furrowed and his grip tightened in his hair. "No, no, I did have a choice. At least I think I did. Did I have a choice? I must have; I should have controlled myself. What is a bit of yelling compared to draining the life of something just so that you feel better? I am going mad, I knew it. This is what I am now. A mad man who kills things to quiet the voices, oh god."

Asman whimpered and tugged at his hair harder, the pain only making more tears worm their way down his face.

"Asman, this is only what you are making of it. You are not mad, but you will be if you let it become so. The spirits will call for you, but you need to ignore them even if they scream. Death Magic can be comforting once you learn to control it."

Niallen's voice was calm, but had a bit of sternness to it that Asman was all too familiar with.

He did not know if he could resist those voices again. They had been so loud and demanding of him, it almost felt easier to give them what they wanted.

"You also do not have to go through this alone. We will help you along the way, dear heart."

Asman inhaled shakily at Dahlias voice from his side, her tone sweet and concerned.

He would never forgive himself if he lost control and killed her. What if he did not know it was even happening? If it was the middle of the night and his magic leaked from him, murdering her and all the other Guards.

With another weak hum he shook his head, closing his eyes again. If he could not see that the Guard were all looking at him then maybe it would make his anxiety lessen.

"Why? Why is this all happening to me? What did I do wrong? Is it because I do not believe in God? He is punishing me for not thinking he is real, or maybe because I prefer men, or because I was weak and could not help Sam. He saw that I did not believe and so he gave me to Vanien so that he may fill my mind with voices and drive me to kill."

Asman shook slightly, his hands itching it hit something. So then he drew them out of his hair and pounded the edge of his fist into his skull, continuing to do so until there were four hands pulling his arms to his sides.

"Just kill me. Please, I am not strong enough for this. I thought I could do it but I cannot. I do not want to hurt anyone, just kill me before I completely loose it and end up executing someone who does not deserve it." Asman struggled against Niallen and Dhalias hands, his eyes still shut but knowing even then there were tears rolling down his face.

"Shh, Asman, there is no need for that. If you do not believe in this God then he can do nothing to hurt you. What is happening now is not your fault in the least, but you need to calm down or you will hurt yourself." Niallen huffed as Asman pushed hard and the man had to slam his arm back down.

"Why are you even here? I am supposed to be angry with you, fucking arse!" Asman opened his eyes finally to send Niallen a glare. He was still struggling, but it did nothing against the muscled arms holding him.

"You can continue to be angry with me as long as you prolong this endeavor. I am not going to let you get hurt just because you think you deserve it, Asman." Niallen growled lightly, his grip tightening even though the man beneath them had slowed in his escape due to fatigue.

Asman frowned and sniffed, his breath coming in soft pants as his body rebelled against him. The tears had at least slowed while he listened to the man.

He glanced over the Guard, all sitting there even though most of them had turned to talk quietly amongst themselves. Some were still watching him though, with looks of sadness and worry that had Asman furrowing his brows.

Why did they care about him? They had known him for barely a week yet they still looked at him like he was someone to be cared about.

"I do not know how to control it." Asman whispered, his voice scared and embarrassed.

"That is alright. We will help you learn and figure out how to use it without anybody or thing getting hurt." Dahlia stayed easily with a shake of her head.

Asman nodded tightly and pressed his lips together. He had stopped struggling, but Niallen and Dhalia's hands remained at his arms. They were gentle enough that Asman did not mind all that much.

He exhaled shakily and then took a deep breath, finally hearing that it was still raining outside.

The raindrops were still making noise against the canvas, but Asman found himself not minding as much as he did before. It was instead almost soothing the way that he could listen to the gentle dripping of water into a puddle nearby. The frogs still sang out near the pond, though they quickly filtered out of Asman's mind seeing as he did not focus on them for long.

He felt Dahlias thumb rub softly against him arm and he sighed, shutting his eyes as the exhaustion hit him dead on.

Asman slowly let his breathing die down, his eyes becoming heavier even if they were already shut.

The hands on his arms never left, but he did feel one of his hands be filled with another, though he was unsure of which side it came from as he fell deeper into the blackness.

Asman did not know when he woke next, but when he did he was alone in the tent.

He had flipped onto his side during the night, so when he had opened his eyes he was met with an empty tent and the sound of cicadas.

The rain was gone at least, though Asman could still smell the rain and soil in the air.

With a grunt, he managed to lift himself off of the ground, the blankets that had once been on him were pushed off to the side.

He stumbled at first, finding that his head was a bit dizzy as he stood. Asman remembered all of what had happened an unknown amount of time ago, but it was hazy in his mind; as if he had a few ales too many.

Asman tried to find his water canteen, but it seemed as if everything had been moved from the tent except for him.

With fawn-like legs, he walked over to the tent entrance and drew open the flap, nearly being blinded from how bright the sun was outside.

After allowing his eyes to adjust, he carefully stepped outside and made a noise in the back of his throat when the sun touched his chest, warming it even more than it already was.

The Guard was thankfully outside when Asman came out. All of them were standing around a singular fire with smiles as they laughed over what was likely a comment someone made, though all heads turned when he stepped into the open.

Dahlia was the first to come forward, offering his canteen and shirt back to him with a smile.

Asman took them both gratefully and gave his own tight lipped smile, keeping his eyes down as to not meet them with someone and see the pity theres held.

He came forward a bit to join the circle before slipping on his tunic, ignoring the stares while he came to stand in between Dahlia and Niallen.

The man did not say anything to him, though he did call out for Jacksill, Stulvon, and Dahlia to start taking the tent down. Asman felt as if he needed to help, but the unsteady legs beneath him called for him to stay put.

"How are you feeling?" Niallen finally asked after a moment. The Guard had gone back to their chatter after the leader had spoke.

"Unsteady." Asman huffed and tipped the canteen back to drink the water inside. There was not much left from before, so it only took a few broad gulps for the liquid to be gone.

"You should eat some before we leave. I believe I have some dried fish if you would like some?" Niallen offhandedly began reaching down to pick up a bag, the soft crackling of the fish coming from it.

Asman blanched and shook his head lightly, putting a hand up to stop the man.

"No, no, that is alright. I am not actually that hungry at the moment." Asman grimaced and sighed when Niallen put the bag back down. "I only... I wanted to apologize for how I behaved while I was awake; I was confused and not right in the head and I am sorry for being so difficult."

Niallen furrowed his brows and looked at Asman with a contemplative stare.

"Asman, there is nothing to be sorry for in the least. I will not deny that you were troubled yesterday, but it was only due to the stress of everything that has happened to you. The Voices of the Dead is something that all Death Magic users have trouble with, and it only takes you not wanting to do what they say for you to take control of the situation." Niallen glanced around briefly before sighing, "I realize that I had told you I wanted to wait till we reached Isadren to explain things, but I fear that not knowing will only put you in harms way. I should like you to ride with me today so I can fill you in."

Asman frowned and sighed gently before nodding, his eyes falling to the grass as his boots became littered in dewdrops.

"It might also benefit for me to apologize." Niallen's face twisted slightly; Asman could not tell if it was because he did not want to do so or if he was embarrassed. "I should not have reacted the way

I did towards you going to bed with someone. It worries me when my Guard goes to sleep somewhere away, but that should not be an excuse to intrude on your personal life. You have shown that you are capable of protecting yourself when you feel threatened, and I will try not to make another mistake like that again."

Asman inhaled sharply, his breath catching in his throat as he turned to stare at Niallen. He did not know if he preferred the man to be cold, as when he was it was easier to disregard his good looks for a poor personality. Now, Asman cursed his face for heating while the man showed a good trait hidden beneath the rough lining of a leader.

"I... Thank you." Asman whispered as he averted his eyes back to the ground, his arms coming to cross against his chest.

There was much he wanted to say back to the man; how Asman was only mad because he did not feel like he was a part of the Guard, or that Niallen was truly a good leader he was sorry for ever assuming littler of him.

But all that came out was a hum as he was unable to form the words.

It almost seemed too good to be true, what Niallen was implying. He so easily put Asman in the same grouping of the Guard, the same grouping that he worried about when they were gone for the night.

Asman had never been someone to be cared for like this. It had always been that he was the boy that did not have parents and spent too much time with the merchants and bards, he had too much of a liking towards history or philosophy and not enough for butchering and making a living.

The girls who liked him only did so because of his appearance, though once they finally knew him they backed away and rarely spoke to him.

How did Asman know that the Guard would not do the same?

They had been welcoming enough so far, but none of them knew who he was besides a broken man with Death Magic and voices in his head. Would they, after a certain point, think he was strange for them also?

If anything happened again like yesterday, would they deem him a threat to others?

Yesterday. It had already been a day since Asman had gone mad underneath all their gazes. He had already proven how unstable he was.

How long until he completely lost his head?

How long until they take back their quickly placed trust?

Chapter Twelve: Sight

The Guard did not wait long to begin traveling once more.

Asman did not exactly know the time when they left, but he could assume that since the sun was lower in the sky, it was still morning.

His legs were still sore, so it felt nice sitting in the saddle finally with Niallen. He was not tied this time, but the man still put him in front so that Asman could hear him better.

With everything packed and the Guard on their horses, they set off back on the road towards Isadren.

The sun was shining, but there seemed to be a cooler breeze, so at least Asman would not be too warm today.

The forest was lively, with the birds and frogs singing and the flora flush and green. The storm had given everything a boost of life that perked it all up; but Asman was almost uncomfortable at all the life. He ignored the feeling for now, not wanting a repeat of the other night, and instead listened as Niallen began his explanation.

"How much do you know about magic, Asman?"

Asman hummed as he settled back against the man and his fingers found Berrys mane, where there were still six little braids hanging delicately by blades of grass.

"Nothing useful I am afraid. We were taught that magic was the work of Vanien and that if we saw anybody use it to tell an adult. Though, I do not think anybody in Thamor actually had any magic." Asman shrugged, his eyes flitting around casually to stare at the view the road provided.

"I do not know much about the Feliasian God, only enough to know that in my opinion his followers stance on magic is often misguided through ignorance." Niallen sighed gently and Asman felt it ruffle his hair. "People who truly know magic or use it could tell just how beautiful and useful it can be.

"There are many types of magic, but there are those that are more common; such as Ritual or Moon Magic. Queen Kelnua has Natural Magic, the kind that draws from nature and the magic that is always in the air. She does not use it much, only to keep in contact with us and sometimes for political issues." Niallen spoke gently, and Asman could tell that he had brought Berry further up from the rest of the group. "Teran's Water Magic is similar and the same amount of common as Natural Magic. Water, Fire, Earth, Air, and Metallurgy Magic all fall under the title of Elemental. They are the least rare and the users do not often become that strong. Teran has exceptional strength, but he could never overthrow nature, those are the rules with all Elemental Mages."

Asman hummed to show he was listening. This was was all very fascinating to him; the different types of magic that those can have and the way that somehow the users could not succeed past nature.

"The magic that includes the Moon or Sun is a little more complex and rare; those who use it have to devote their life to it. Though it is still common enough that almost every Guard has someone they know with it.

"Healing Magic is just another way of saying Life Magic, but those who practice it are normally few and far between due to the high demand for them. They often stay in the palace or go to the front lines, so there are not many." Niallen paused briefly and collected his thoughts. "Death Mages and Shadow Mages are both the rarest to come by. With how dangerous their magic is at points, it is an unfortunate truth that the power could go to their head easily."

Asman frowned but kept silent, wishing to know whatever Niallen had to say as it would perhaps help with the conflict happening within his mind. His fingers wrapped idly around a lock of Berrys mane, listening carefully while Niallen made to continue.

"From what I have learned in the past, Shadow Magic is a difficult magic to control; the light and dark do not always listen, and sometimes they listen too well and the user has issues retreating from the shadows. The Mage could get stuck in a shadow and once it disappears in the sun, then the Mage does too." Niallen took a deep breath. "My sister had Shadow Magic. She... got distracted during a battle and could not see that the sun was rising."

Asman shifted a bit, his frown tightening for a moment. Niallen lost his sister just as Asman had lost Sam.

The man stayed silent for a moment; likely lost in his thoughts. Asman could understand, as he himself was still grieving his brother.

"Anyway, there is a similar caution one has to use when having Shadow or Death Magic. You and other Death Mages are seen as dangerous only because of what the magic does to you." Niallen sighed softly, his breath tickling the back of Asman's neck. "Death Mages are in tune with the Dead. They can hear them and often are driven to insanity by this. Your kind are so rare that I am afraid I do not know much about them besides, many have used their magic to cause chaos instead of something good. Having a good stance within your head in imperative so that the Dead do not overwhelm you and coerce you to do something you do not want."

"Is there anything positive about this magic?" Asman questioned with a light huff.

"I am sorry, but I do not know. I was only taught enough to keep the Guard safe. The Queen never saw this happening unfortunately."

Asman sighed and nodded, still staring off at the green surrounding the road. It felt like everything was watching him, waiting for him to snap again.

"Could you tell me about Isadren?" Asman asked after a moment. "I can only assume that the things I have been taught are false, and I can only learn so much from merchants and bards that do not live there."

Niallen chuckled softly and pulled Berry's reins so that the mare would slow down enough to join the group once more.

"It is beautiful. I lived further west than the Capital, so my family home was stationed in the Mattonel Mountains. Every morning you would wake and step out to see the entirety of Isadren below you. It is always cool, but there are times in the summer when the snow melts and the land becomes green with life." Niallen trailed off before clearing his throat. "The people there are some of the best I have ever met. There is not much prejudice when it comes to skin color or race; of course there are always those who disapprove, but they are often taken care of by the others in the town. Isadren still has trouble with people accepting those that have no gender, such as Elsten and Danyel. People are still too small minded to fully welcome them, though I am proud to say that those that like the same sex are almost fully equal to those who do not. You obviously do not have any aversion towards those of the same sex."

Asman blushed and chuckled nervously a bit, his hand tightening slightly in Berry's mane.

"No. No, I do not." He exhaled lightly, staring down to where there was a dragonfly resting on his leg. "I... When you told me that you knew, I was scared that you would react poorly to who I was with, rather than what I had done. It is silly, I know. Especially since Dahlia told me the Guard does not care about those things, but Felias does and I spent my whole life hiding who I was with when I snuck away for a night."

"It would be unfair of me to judge you for what gender you prefer, since I am partial to men also." Niallen spoke and Asman could hear the smirk in his voice.

"You like men too?" Asman questioned quickly, his heartbeat quickening for a reason he did not care to admit.

"Yes, and women, and those in between. I was raised to appreciate someone's beauty regardless of what is in their trousers, even though I can appreciate that specific beauty as well." Niallen's voice was teasing almost, and it did nothing to help Asman's situation.

Just like before, he was having trouble not allowing his heart to grow fond. The man was not being as irritating lately, and showing how his personality truly was. Asman was left feeling helpless to his own emotions; what would happen if these feelings stood in the way of him bettering himself?

Asman could not cross this line when there was so much to do on the side his feet were planted in. The goals that he needed to reach did not include pining after a man he had met a week ago and getting distracted from what was at stake.

"Well, I am glad that I do not have to worry about hiding who I am." Asman smiled also, though it only stayed on his face for a short while. "How much longer until we reach Isadren?"

"A fortnight till we reach the border, after that it will only be another week for the Capital." Niallen hummed and shrugged against Asman's body. "I should probably begin teaching you swordwork tonight. The Isadren and Felias border is almost always guarded, and we cannot cut through Sedrey for account of there being no road, so there is a chance we will have to fight our way home."

Niallen's body language changed so fast that Asman could smell the shift in the air. He body was still as lax as it had been, but there was a more serious tone to the air.

"How did you get into Felias in the first place?"

"We sailed along the Sedrey Islands and entered through one of the ports near their Capital. From there we rode into Felias as Sedrey Nomads. Unfortunately, the trip would be too long for us to do once more." Niallen explained easily.

"What did you do while you were here? I mean, I know the Guard collected information, but what type of information is important enough to spend so much time behind enemy lines?" Asman asked, watching as Berry shook her head and the dragonfly that was still standing on him flew away.

"You would be surprised how many Feliasian soldiers know about where they attack next, and how loose lipped they can be in the company of women." Niallen inhaled slowly. "This was one of the shorter excursions actually. I have gone on many over the years, one of them almost reaching four winters. These missions give enough information to the Queen that when the time comes, the army is ready to fight back. I am proud in what we have done and at how many lives we have saved."

"Do you not have family in Isadren that you miss?" Asman frowned slightly; he could not imagine leaving Sam for so long by choice, though he supposed that did not matter now.

"Yes, but the Guard is my family too. Though, some of them have partners and children back home. Their families understand, but it can sometimes be taxing to not speak to your loved ones for years on end."

Asman glanced over to his side and behind, where the Guard were talking and laughing, showing no signs of homesickness even if they had been away for nearly a year.

"Some do not have family to go back to. Those who are not Isadrenians do not have their family anymore, besides Finnet and Vanora. They are like you, in that way." Niallen spoke quietly at the last sentence, his voice soft.

Asman turned back around and planted his fingers in Berry's mane once more, pulling a section out to begin braiding.

"I think there has been so much going on that I have not thought about it." Asman whispered, tucking the hair in and out behind itself.

"Sometimes it is not good to dwell on things. You are mourning in your own way and there is little you can do to help that. You thought of him when I healed you, and you have decided to avenge him. I believe that is as much as you can do at the moment." Niallen said just as softly as Asman.

"I keep forgetting that I am not just on a trip and that I will go back to him once this is over. I will not ever see him again."

Asman's lip quivered slightly as tears made there way to his eyes.

"I know you are not religious, Asman. But I should like to think that you will see him when it is your time. Most Isadrenians believe that when you die, you will continue to live as your best self in the Hall of Grethen with those who you have loved."

"What if because of this magic I do not go anywhere good when I die? What if there is nothing but pain after death?" Asman sniffed and paused in his braid to wipe his eyes, regaining his composure.

"You still have a long time yet before there is a decision to be made. Perhaps you could think of your brother when you become too overwhelmed by The Dead. Think that if he loved you, he would not want to see you like that. I did not know him, but if he was anything like you, I can tell that he would hate to see you break." Niallen rested his hands on Asman's thighs, the reins still dangling from his fists.

Asman chuckled wetly, rubbing his nose and sniffing again before returning to his braid.

"He would. Sam always hated seeing me cry, he said it was because I was an ugly crier. But he would still coax me from the tree and make me tell him what was wrong." Asman laughed at the memory of Sam flicking his red nose and saying that no woman would ever fuck him if he cried all the time; the smile plastered to his face even as he said such things.

"Do you always climb trees when you are upset?" Niallen asked lightly, a smirk once again lilting through his words.

"Most of the time, yes. I began doing it after my father died and Sam hated it because I would not come down even to eat, so he would sometimes throw blueberries at me until I came down. He never really liked our father due to how much the man pushed him to be a good butcher, but I was always close with him, so it hurt when he passed." Asman had healed over the many years that had gone by since his fathers death, so talking about him was no issue. "There still times throughout the years after I had a bad day, I would climb the tallest tree I could find and listen to the leaves in the wind. It was soothing."

"I do not think I could ever climb a tree too high." Niallen sighed out a laugh. "I am frightened of heights."

The man spoke lowly as he confessed to Asman his fear, but the other man just laughed lightly.

"You would not think a man like you would have many fears." Asman chimed, but still kept his voice quiet so that the other Guards would not hear.

"A man like me?" Niallen inquired tauntingly and Asman flushed.

"Large, demanding, the leader of a group that specifically invades an enemy kingdom to get information for a Queen." Asman shrugged, a smile pulling at his lips easily.

"What? Are you saying you do not have fears also? It is a natural human response. Besides, I did not grow up climbing trees or looking over cliffs, so I have not been exposed to facing heights often." Niallen huffed haughtily.

"Of course I have fears, just not of heights. If you see me near a moth you might understand why I have no more room in my body for any more fear." Asman shuddered at just the thought of the furry flying fucks.

"Moths? You are scared of a small bug?" Niallen questioned and Asman bristled.

"I will have you know that moths can be large, almost as large as my hand! They fly at you and stick and eat at your clothes; they are disgusting little beasties and I hate them." Asman huffed sharply, but there was still a small smile on his face.

"I suppose when you spend as much time in the woods as I have, you learn to not care as much about the beasties." Niallen laughed lightly.

Asman snickered at the man and undid the small braid in Berry's mane, just so that he could start over again.

He preferred talking to Niallen like this, with no magic or war speeches. Just a casual conversation about things that they had not known about each other.

Asman doubted it would last long, but it was still nice while it lasted. It made him see that perhaps it would actually be okay in the future.

It made him see a spot amongst these people just for him.

Chapter Thirteen: Metal

Days passed easily and without fanfare from then on.

Niallen stayed true to his word and began teaching Asman how to wield a sword. They would practice for a few hours before dark while Asman attempted to keep up with the man.

It had taken almost two evenings for Asman to be able to actually wield the sword correctly, and nearly seven more for him to finally feel comfortable striking. Niallen had said he was quick to learn, but Asman felt as if it took ages and many more bruises than needed.

Of course, Niallen thought it best to use an actual sword and not a branch while Asman began. This resulted in many more cuts than needed also.

There had been one instance that Asman forgot to block one of Niallen's advances, and the night ended in the former having to be stitched up by Hilcren once more. Niallen apologized, but only after telling Asman that he needed to work on his dodges if he was unable to block.

Even though Asman took the advice and was able to block the next time, it certainly made Asman pause in his ever constant feelings for the man.

There was no doubt in his mind that Niallen was attractive; especially when the Guard had stopped at a small lake and Asman had got to see the man with his hair down and wet. But, there was a doubt as to if the man even cared about Asman besides as just another Guard.

When Asman would watch Niallen interact with the others, it was in almost the exact same way as he would do with Asman.

At some points, Asman was almost glad with this, seeing that Niallen was enough of a good leader to not have favor for someone more than the others. But again, did this mean that Asman needed to rethink his feelings to be more practical?

He had tried talking to Dahlia about it, but they only had so much alone time before either one was needed for something or Asman was required for more training.

So, even though it had been just past a fortnight since Asman had started traveling with them, he was still at a standstill with how to feel.

Besides his swordsmanship and feelings of Niallen, he had also been practicing with Teran to gain better control of his magic.

Asman, at first, wanted nothing to do with it. He was terrified that if he became too overwhelmed, he could accidentally put someone else in danger. Though, after Niallen, Dahlia, and Teran each spoke to him about the risk being low if no one was around, Asman begrudgingly said yes.

He mostly practiced alone, at night, far off from camp just in case something bad did happen.

The hard part was not letting the magic out, but instead focusing it on one thing and then drawing it back in.

The voices of The Dead still called loudly for Asman to continue until nothing was left, and the first time he practiced, Asman nearly did give in. That is, until he repeated to himself many times over that Sam would not want him to give in, and that it was not The Dead's Magic, but his own. Who would he be if he could not control his own magic?

The next few times after that, Teran joined him and showed Asman his own magic.

It was not much, but the small clouds of mist or drops of water were entertaining and made Asman feel better that he was not the only one with magic.

Teran helped him begin focusing his magic on smaller things; blades of grass, little flowers or weeds, and bugs that would crawl on them while they sat against trees or in meadows.

Each night, Asman got just a little bit better at controlling the outflow of magic and quieting the voices.

At one of the sparse larger villages they stayed in, Niallen bought Asman a horse of his own so that Berry would not have to carry so much each day.

Asman had tried to deny that he needed a horse at all, and that if him riding Berry was a problem then he could walk, but Niallen had been insistent that Asman walking would only slow them down.

So then that was how Asman ended up with Cedran, a black and white gelding that luckily did not hate Asman.

Niallen had to teach him the commands for a horse, but even then Cedran mostly followed the others. Asman was nervous having his own animal to care after, and even if he had ridden Berry, he was still uneasy around such a large beast.

Asman still did not know where Niallen and the Guard got the coin they had, since every time he asked Niallen said it was unimportant. Asman still had the three coins from the bard that had pitied him in Stelai, so once Niallen paid for Cedran, it felt nice to shove the small amount of money into the mans hand regardless of his attempts to give them back.

From then on, the days were the same; ride until dusk, train with swords until night, train his magic with Teran, and then sleep until morning and repeat the day over.

On the eighteenth day of their journey, Asman could tell that they were getting closer to the border. There were no more villages as far as he could tell, and there had not been any for at least a few nights before.

It was colder now also, even as Niallen and him trained, Asman was shivering every so often from the wind. Luckily for him, Dahlia had given him a simple cotton cloak to keep him warm, but while sparring with Niallen the fabric would only get in the way.

Their training did not last long that evening, seeing as Asman had nearly fully figured out the moves necessary for sword fighting.

Niallen was also quick to retreat to his tent after training, saying something about a letter he had to read.

Asman easily dismissed this and joined back up with the rest of the Guard, throwing his sword- which Niallen lent him,- down onto his bedroll.

Dahlia already had a bowl of broth, mushrooms, and potatoes, waiting for him when he finally sat down in the grass around the fire. Asman immediately pulled on his cloak and drank down the warm liquid to try and leech the cold from his bones.

The Guard seemed closer to him now also; more willing to joke with him or pull him into stories that he had not heard before. It made Asman content to know that the people he had been around for such a long time were comfortable with him regardless of his past or magic.

They laughed when he told jokes, and made sure he had a spot near the fire, since most everyone knew that he was not used to the cold.

The Silvanian and Galdren Guards had been to Isadren before, and were more accustomed to the cold than Asman. They had told him they were the same way the first time they finally breached the border.

Asman was dreading and also excited to see Isadren. The cold would likely be something he would not like, though he was looking forward to seeing the snow.

Where he was in Felias, it rarely snowed, and only ever did so for a short time until the flakes melted in the water puddles and mud. It was childish, but Asman would like to play in the snow for once.

"Niallen has not come out to eat yet."

Asman turned to Dahlia, finding her eyes glancing suspiciously over to the mans tent.

"He said he had to read a letter, I am sure he is just responding." Asman shrugged lightly, tipping back the last bit of broth in his bowl.

"Sure, but he does not usually take this long. The sun has already set." Dahlia frowned, nodding to where the sky was differing shades of pink and blue, the sun long behind the horizon.

"I could bring him some food, if that will calm your nerves?" Asman suggested easily; it had actually been longer than what Niallen normally took to finish his work.

"Please? I know he is likely just too focused on the letters, but he should not miss out on meals. He has already begun cutting back the amount he eats." Dahlia grimaced and used her own bowl to ladle more stew into.

Asman took the bowl from her after setting his own down and standing.

"I will make sure he eats, Dahlia." He assured, patting her head gently and setting off towards the mans tent.

The Guards all gave various forms of telling him to be careful, as interrupting Niallen while he was writing was something no one ever did.

Asman ignored the remarks and only lifted his hand to ruffle the tent flap a little.

"Niallen? I brought dinner." Asman called and after waiting a few moments for an answer, frowned and stepped inside.

Niallen was sitting at his desk, like Asman thought he would be, but the man was staring off absently. His hair had pieces dangling from the edges, as if Niallen had not bothered to regather his hair since training.

Even as Asman walked inside, Niallen did not look over, his eyes still glued to the corner of the tent.

"Niallen? Are you alright?" Asman stepped forward cautiously. He still did not budge. "Niallen. Niallen!"

The man finally snapped from his thought and looked to Asman, his brows furrowed as he cleared his throat and looked back to the desk to begin arranging the papers there.

"Please leave, Asman." Niallen stated in a calm voice, though the other man could tell that something was wrong.

"I brought you food. You were late to dinner." Asman huffed, stepping forward just enough to hold out the bowl to Niallen. "What is wrong? What was in that letter?"

"Thank you for the food, Asman, but I would appreciate it if you left me to think in piece." Niallen took the bowl and immediately set it down on the desk, his jaw clenched right enough that Asman could see the muscle twitch.

"I am not leaving until I know you have eaten, unfortunately. Dahlia wanted me to make sure you did so." Asman crossed his arms defiantly.

Niallen shut his eyes and sighed irritably. Asman resisted the urge to flinch when the man stood up and glared at him.

"I will eat when I damn please. I do not need you in here hovering while I think." Niallen grit out, his hands coming to rest offensively on the desk.

"Why are you getting upset? I am only trying to make sure you do not starve yourself. Now, what was in that letter that has you thinking so hard?" Asman furrowed his brows while he tried to keep himself from getting angry.

"It does not matter right now. If I eat will you fucking go?" Niallen growled out and Asman could have laughed; he was not afraid of Niallen.

Asman shrugged in answer, because truly, he was not leaving until he found out what was in that letter or was physically removed from the tent.

Niallen scoffed and sat down, keeping eye contact with Asman while he gulped down the broth and filled his cheeks with mushrooms and potatoes.

Asman raised an eyebrow at the other mans squirrel like cheeks but angry expression.

When all the food was swallowed at once and a dribble of broth was wiped away, Niallen stared up at Asman expectedly.

"Will you leave now?" He asked harshly and Asman tilted his head.

"What was in the letter?" Asman countered easily while he glanced to said letter on the desk.

It was easy to distinguish since Niallen left the wax seals on the newest letters. There had been little explained to him, but Asman knew that somehow the Queen was able to send the letters and receive them in a leather bag that matched with Niallen's.

"Nothing of importance just yet. Asman, I need to think and you are not helping." Niallen sighed and broke eye contact just to scrub a hand over his face.

In the split second that Niallen was not watching though, Asman snatched the letter up and bolted from the tent.

"Asman! You little fucker-"

He heard Niallen yelling from the tent, but the sound drifted as he ran out and past the Guards towards a large pine tree.

Asman shoved the parchment between his teeth at the seal and immediately began hoisting his body up onto the lowest branch. He could hear Niallen coming up behind him quickly, so it was a rush to pull himself up and further between the branches.

The tree was large enough that Asman would be able to get fairly high without any limbs breaking.

He glanced downwards once to see Niallen with a pissed off look as he kicked the base of the tree. Asman knew the man would not follow him, especially not so high.

When Asman finally found a stable and comfortable looking spot, he sat down on the branch and sighed. His breath was coming out in short pants from climbing so fast.

The wax seal that had been in his mouth had the imprint of teeth marks on it now, and Asman felt bad for that until he actually began to read the letter.

His breath hitched and his brows furrowed while he read. Asman's bitterness toward Niallen grew with each word written on in the letter.

Asman was not that well of a reader, but he could still make out enough of the words to realize what was happening just two days north of them.

With a grumble, he began to descend from the tree, nearing closer to Niallen's impatient pacing and crossed arms.

Asman easily leaped down from the branches, landing right in front of Niallen. The man immediately opening his mouth to say something before Asman cut him off.

"How could you say this was not of importance, Niallen? This effects every one of us; why you did not announce this the moment you got it is baffling to me." Asman huffed and shoved the letter back at Niallen harshly. "There are only two days to the border, how do you expect us to ready for a battle without even knowing about it?"

"Ready for battle? Asman, you read that letter. We are far too outnumbered to bring a group of only twenty five to a war zone." Niallen stared back at Asman as if he was crazy.

"You would rather sit on our arses while Felias gains a foothold in Isadren? They are already over the river. The letter stated that there were only three hundred men fighting for Felias; two hundred Isadrenians must have cut that number down drastically."

"I would rather not send people into a fruitless death. We do not know exactly how many Feliasian soldiers remain, and I would prefer to know that prior to walking onto a battlefield." Niallen's voice was hard, yet quiet as to not give away the subject of their converstaion to the rest of the Guards.

Asman growled low in his throat and shook his head in disbelief.

"You promised me that Felias would get their dues for what they did to Thamor. I will not stand idly by while the army continues to wreak havock upon Calia. You may be a coward; take the Guard west to Sedrey and avoid the battle all together, but I am going to continue north and fight." Asman pushed once more to Niallen's chest before stalking past the man.

Asman pulled the cloak closer together under the chilled wind, walking quickly over to where the Guard were still sitting around the fire and staring at the encounter.

He only got maybe halfway before there was a hand at his wrist pulling him back to face Niallen once more.

"I do not care if you continue north, but do not ever call me a coward, Asman. I am responsible for twenty three other lives besides yours. It is not always what I want, but what needs to happen as to keep these people safe so they can return to their families." Niallen spoke harshly, his face closer to Asman's than it had ever been.

Asman ripped his wrist from Niallen's grip easily, not backing down from the glare Niallen had placed him under.

"They are their own people too, Niallen. Do not act as if they are children who cannot make their own decisions. Tell them what is happening and ask them." Asman sighed, giving up on glaring and stepping back a tad. "If the Feliasian army is too large, we can reconsider. Though there are ways we can still diminsh their numbers; hide in the trees and take the long range attack. I realize that some may not want to fight, but I will not throw away a chance to get revenge on as many soldiers as possible before I die."

Niallen huffed and looked down at the ground, shaking his head before giving a sharp laugh.

"How is it you know so much about battle strategies being a butcher for a small village?" Niallen asked as his face softened from the tight and annoyed one it had been before.

"Common sense, I suppose. The men in the village were all told to prepare to be drafted; there are things you think about when told such things." Asman shrugged, turning back once more to start off towards the Guard.

This time, there was no hand to grab him back and only Niallen's footsteps following him.

Asman easily sat back down near the fire, close enough that he sighed at the warmth it provided. He reached for a blanket to throw around his shoulders while Niallen stepped up to face the group.

It was their decision to make, but the Guards decision likely would be the difference between Asman dying or not.

Chapter Fourteen: Spirit

With no surprise to Asman, the Guard chose to fight.

Some of the members had of course been hesitant after Niallen's speech to them, yet there was no question that the Guard still wanted to fight.

Asman was relieved to find that he would not be fighting alone, but the look that Niallen gave him after the decision was made greatly diminished his mood for the night. The mans face was contorted in a way that said 'Whatever happens is your fault.'

He tried not to dwell on the look for long while the Guard finally laid down to sleep.

The firelight was warm and flickering across the grass as Asman lay on his bedroll. His eyes were lidded and watching his own fingers while they danced across blades of grass, killing them as they went.

Asman sighed softly and finally shut his eyes, letting sleep easily claim him after the long day.

"Asman... Asmannn. Wake up Asman, do not not want to see what you have done?"

The voice faded in and out around Asman's head, the mans eyes snapping open to try and see where it was coming from. Instead though, he found a black starless sky staring back down at him.

"Look around, Asman. This is all your fault, you wanted them to fight, did you not?"

Asman sat up and did as told, glancing around at the carnage that was laid before him.

The Guard was dead, all lying on the ground with unbreathing forms.

Next to him, Dahlia was laid out with open and dead eyes. When Asman looked closer, he could see her throat slit, deep red blood gushing from the wound.

"No, no, no, how did this happen?" Asman whispered, reaching out to try and stop the bleeding, even though he knew she was already gone.

"You did this, Asman. You wanted everyone to fight with you, and this is what happened. Not that it was not going to happen anyway; you are mad, who is to say you would not have killed them after you finally lost it?"

The Voice became louder while it floated closer to Asman's ears. He inhaled sharply and let go of Dahlia to shove his hands over his head.

"I did not do this. I know I did not, you are lying. I would never kill my friends." Asman growled out, his words sounding funny due to the palms over his ears.

He could feel the blood from Dahlias wound stick to his skin, the smell thick and of iron. Asman had tears forming in his eyes; Dahlia was dead, the Guard was dead.

"Oh? Look behind you. Is that not how you would kill him?"

Asman's eyes widened as he unclaspes his hands and turned around, his heartbeat stuttering at the sight.

It was Niallen this time, his neck bruised blue and purple. Asman felt sick to his stomach looking at him like that; his hair splayed across the grass, eyes wide and red and unseeing, neck mangled by hands that he had trusted.

Asman whimpered and shook his head, holding a hand to his mouth at the sudden need to expel his stomach.

"This is not real. I would not do this." He exhaled shakily, the tears now flowing harshly across his cheeks.

"You can not control yourself, Asman. Killing plants and bugs will never be enough for you. You finally broke and killed every single one of your friends. The people that trusted you and laughed with you, dead because of you. Your brother died because you did not protect him-"

"S-stop. He was killed by a Feliasian soldier. I could not do anything, I-"

"-watched as a man slit his throat. Just as you did to poor Dahlia; her blood is on your hands, Asman. Niallen's too, what do you think he was thinking when you squeezed the life from his body? Do you think he regretted it all? Regretted letting you get close enough to snuff out his light?"

Asman continued to shake his head, bringing his hands back up to clutch at his ears.

"I did not kill them. I know I did not kill them. It was the battle that did so. The battle that... that I wanted them to fight in. I wanted them to fight with me... I-I led them to their deaths."

"You did, Asman. Say it. Say you killed them -

Asman's breathing quickened, the feeling in his heart was sickening while he stared at both Dahlia and Niallen's dead bodies. The scent in the air was sweet, and even though Asman new it was the smell of death, he almost like the stench.

"I... I killed-"

"Asman!"

Said man looked around quickly; that was not The Voice. That sounded like Dahlia, but she was in front of him dead.

"Asman, wake up!" Dahlias voice shouted once more and Asman shook his head.

"No. No, she is not alive. You are fucking with my mind, she is dead!" He yelled off into the darkness at The Voice, who was suspiciously quiet now.

"Asman, you need to wake up."

That was Niallen's voice.

"Stop. Stop! Quit messing with me, I know they are dead. I killed them!" Asman sobbed harshly, listening as The Voice finally began laughing.

"No, you did not. But you will. When you eventually give in to us, you will kill everyone you care for. Just as those soldiers did bef-"

Asman gasped as he jolted up and awake, water dripping down his face and filling his lungs.

He instantly started to cough and inhale greedy breaths, his heart still pounding from what was apparently a dream. There were tears mixing with the water on his face, but he was unsure if they were already there or if they were residual from before.

There were hands at his shoulders, and when he opened his eyes and glanced over he found Dahlia and Niallen at his sides.

With a sob, he pulled himself free and quickly stood on shaky legs. Asman stumbled away from the camp only for a second before he was brought to his knees and began vomiting.

The stench from before still lingered in his nose, as if it was all real. But it was not. Because a dream could not feel so real, right?

Asman continued to expel what was in his stomach until there was nothing left and he was only dry heaving painfully. He whimpered and carefully fell down to the side, curling up in a ball to try and comfort himself in some way.

He could still feel his heartbeat in his chest, his mind frazzled while it argued with itself about reality. Was this the dream? Was The

Voice felling the truth? Are Dahlia and Niallen dead? Did Asman kill them?

"Asman? Love, come on, it was only a night terror." Dahlias voice lilted from a short distance away.

Asman only whimpered again and sobbed, the grip on his legs tightening until his forehead was touching his knees.

He was terrified that if he opened his eyes and looked at anyone, they would be dead. He could still hear the dry and rotten tone of The Voice while it mocked him.

"You are not mad. You are not mad. You are not mad." Asman whispered to himself, ignoring the hand that had come to rest on his back.

"Asman. We know you are not mad. Everyone is alive and safe, no one is dead and you did not kill them." Niallen's low voice made Asman shake. The Voice was trying to trick him. The hand on his back was fake.

Asman shivered, but he could not tell if it was because of his emotions or because of the cold. Though, you could not feel cold in a dream, so it must have been his emotions.

"This is real, Asman. You are with the Guard, we are two days from the Isadren and Felias border, it is almost dawn and it is near freezing out." Niallen's voice spoke again, the hand pressing harder into Asman's numb back. "Open your eyes and look around, Asman. Come sit by the fire and you will see that you are not dreaming anymore."

Asman should not do what Niallen's voice was telling him to do. This could be a test to see how well he could ignore The Dead. It would make sense, since they had all been slaughtered in the dream, or reality, Asman did not know.

Though on the other hand, if they were all dead, then for what reason should he remain in control?

Slowly, Asman opened his eyes and unraveled his body, immediately beginning to shiver harshly. He ignored the cold and hesitantly looked behind him, staring straight back into Niallen's eyes.

The mans eyes were not as they were before; they were the same stormy blue as always, and filled with worry. Asman inhaled sharply while more tears flowed down his face.

Asman looked back over to the fire, seeing that Dahlia and the sleeping Guard were all there. He could hear some of them snoring from beside the fire. Dahlia was looking at him with the same worried and sad eyes that Niallen was.

The hand on his back was still there, and Asman could feel the warmth radiating from it. He finally could tell that he was cold, even worse being that he was not shivering anymore.

Asman allowed Niallen to help him as he stood, the hand moving to his arm and standing Asman up.

He swayed and instinctively grabbed Niallen's shoulder, Asman leaning most of his body on the man as it struggled to find its footing and warmth.

There was no possible way that he could be dreaming now. The temperature, Niallen, his surroundings, they all felt too real to be a dream still.

Asman sobbed harshly, but began stumbling towards the fire again. Niallen allowed Asman to hold onto him while they both walked to Dahlia, who had stood up and was ready to help if need be.

"Shh, you are okay. We need to warm you up, dear heart." Dahlia cooed once Asman finally fell into her arms. "Chew this."

Dahlia handed him a sprig of mint, which he popped into his mouth hastily, hoping it would curb the swirling in his stomach. He inhaled and exhaled quickly through the cool burn of the plant, though it was more sluggish than he would have wanted.

Dahlia sat him down on his bedroll that was closer to the fire and threw a fur over his shoulders, rubbing her hands up and down them to try and create friction. Niallen sat down on the other side of Asman and laid a hand on his knee, though the latter immediately grabbed for the hand with both of his own just so that he knew Niallen was still real.

Niallen did not seem to mind and only curled his hand slightly while rubbing a thumb against one of Asman's shaking hands.

Dahlia rubbed his arms and shoulders until likely she tired, though she instead wrapped her arms around him so try and warm Asman up.

Asman shut his eyes and frowned, trying to even out his breathing while the aftershocks of panic went through him. The fire was doing a good job of warming him along with Dahlia, and holding Niallen's hand was comforting to him.

He kept repeating to himself that everyone was alive. That he did not kill them and The Voice was just that of the dead trying to get him to do so. Dahlias arms were around him and Niallen's heartbeat in his hands. The Guard were sleeping peacefully in front of him. They were alive.

During the time it took for him to calm, the sun had decided to rise over the horizon. The sunlight giving that final push for Asman's body to become warm enough.

"Do you want to talk about your dream?" Dahlia whispered near Asman's ear, still holding onto him, but with only one arm around his shoulders instead of two.

"No." He muttered back with a shake of his head, the word getting caught in his throat some.

"Are you sure? It might help you become less afraid." Dahlias frown was evident in her tone.

Asman shook his head again, sighing after letting go of Niallen's hand. He stood up and allowed the fur and Dahlias arm to fall off his shoulders.

"I am fine. We should... we should start getting ready." Asman inhaled deeply, leaving his two friends to instead walk towards the horses.

He ignored what was certainly some worried looks, but continued to Cedran anyway. The horse was awake and grazing happily, letting out a snort when Asman came to pet him.

This had not been the first time that Asman had a nightmare since that night in the village, but it was the first time that it had felt real. It had been the first time that The Voice had appeared also; seeing as The Dead often spoke to him only when he was overwhelmed. Even worse than that, it had been the first dream to ever include the Guard dead.

Asman could not help but think of the reasons why it would happen now. Did his magic somehow predict what would happen in the future? Or was it only what he subconsciously wanted to do in his mind?

He did not like not knowing things, especially when it pertained to his own mind.

After what had happened last night, Asman could have blamed it on guilt for roping the Guard into fighting, but it was almost like he knew there was more to it than that.

The chances that his dream would come true were high; and Asman felt stupid for ever thinking otherwise. He should have never pulled the Guard in on plans that were meant for him alone.

His anger towards Felias has only grown over the many days of knowing the truth of it. Perhaps Isadrenians were biased, but the Sedreys and Silvanians were not, and Asman could perfectly recount all the stories that Dahlia and Pilla had told him of horrific encounters with the Feliasian army.

Everyone in the Guard was that for a reason. Whether or not they wanted to fight for their country, or had personal qualms with Felias, they had their reasons. But Asman's reason was the most clear of them all.

There were not many that had family killed by Felias; those who hated the kingdom did so greatly because of how the king ran things. Asman was the only Guard to have his whole village taken from him by Felias.

It was beginning to seem like Felias was moving to the offensive in their war strategies, and Asman's village was somehow a part of that strategy.

Because of that, Asman knew that he should not have forced the Guard to join him. This was his fight alone, and now he did not know whether or not the Guard was going to die because of this mistake.

"Asman."

He turned away from where he had been stroking Cedrans man, facing Niallen with a frown.

"Niallen." Asman sighed out and crossed his arms.

"You should not bottle your emotions; especially not when you have people who would listen to you. Dahlia does not know what to do to help you. She is worried, Asman." Niallen spoke softly, close enough that he had reached out a hand to pet Cedrans nose.

Asman bristled at his words and turned back to the horses mane, beginning to comb out debris that had settled their.

"I do not need her worry. Nightmares are common in a lot of people, especially those who have seen what I have. They will come and go, but there is nothing that can help that." Asman huffed with a shrug.

"There is something to help, though. Talking about what you see in your dreams can help you process what you are feeling. I do not understand why you can not take advantage of all the friends you have made here. Most everyone here would never mind you talking to them about-"

"Stop talking."

"Excuse me?" Niallen scoffed towards Asman, who now has his hands clenched in Cedrans mane to the point where the braid was probably knotted now.

"You can not act as if these people deserve to have me as a friend. I am the one that made the mistake of wanting them to fight with me. They are all going to die and I do not know if it will be by Felias' hand or mine." Asman shot a desperate look to Niallen. "You want to know how I am feeling? I feel like shite; I have a voice in my head that tells me to kill people and sometimes I feel like I should just so it will shut up. You were right to want to avoid the battle. The uncertainty can get people killed, and I am sorry that I forced your hand, but these people do not deserve to die for something they could avoid altogether."

Niallen was silent for a few moments, giving enough time in between that Asman at first thought he would not speak at all.

"I was not right, Asman. You were, when you said these people should be able to make their own decisions. Even if it is uncertain, they made their choice to join the fight. If any of us die, I know it will not be by your hand, because even though you think you do not deserve them, you know in your mind that they are family.

Dreaming that something will happen does not mean that it will actually occur."

"How do you know that? How do you know I will not go mad and kill everyone; including you?"

"If you actually wanted any of us dead, we would be so already. The voices may taunt you, but you have been strong so far, and I believe you will continue to be. If you are to kill anyone, it will be the Feliasian army."

"Because I am strong?"

"Because you are strong."

Chapter Fifteen: Smell

T he start of the journey to the border was the most uneasy that Asman had ever felt.

The Guard were almost too normal for what they were stepping into; they remained laughing and joking during the traveling, but Asman could feel the weight in his heart every day they neared the battle.

Nobody actually spoke of what they were walking into, but Asman did see some of them training near the same time he did so with Niallen.

Asman's sword work had improved greatly since he began training, but looking over what the other Guards moved like made him rethink how good he actually was.

He could not beat Niallen yet, though he could get some good strikes in, but perhaps that was not enough for how close they were to battle.

Training with Teran had come to a standstill, since Asman knew mostly how to use his magic well. He wondered if he had enough strength to actually kill a soldier.

They had never practiced on anything larger than a grasshopper, and Asman was surely not going to test his limits on anything bigger than that unless they deserved it. He figured, if he could kill a tree in a short amount of time, he could at least kill a few soldiers at best.

Regardless if Asman could kill, it did not mean he wanted to use his magic for such things; that is where the sword training came in.

The two days to the border passed slowly, seeing as they did not leave until the next day. The day after Asman's dream was spent preparing; gathering and sharpening weapons, making sure that everyone had suitable armor, and giving both the horses and the Guards a rest from traveling.

Asman received armor from Stulvon and a newer and sharper sword from Marrion, one of the Isadrenians that was close with Niallen.

The sword was standard, but beautiful in its own simple way. Asman adored how the blade looked in the sun, and how the handle felt in his palm; it felt as if it belonged there.

By the next day, Asman was prepared for battle and weighing down Cedran a tad more. His sword on his hip and leather heavy on his shoulders, the ride was a little less pleasant.

The only thing he could focus on was how Niallen kept sniffing at the air and frowning. Each time the wind blew, or they took a break from walking, Niallen was there with flared nostrils and a hard look.

Asman knew the mans sense of smell was outstanding, and wondered what Niallen was smelling to make him do so that often. He figured he could ask, but there was not any reason to strike a conversation.

Every time that Asman even looked at the man, his heart frazzled in his chest. He was not sure if he could stand not looking at Niallen for more than half a day.

Though, it seemed that the man could do with not looking at Asman for a great deal more time. The only time Niallen ever looked at him was when Asman was speaking to him, making the latter clearly understand the situation.

Besides this revelation, Asman still would look at Niallen casually. If anyone asked, he could easily make up a lie to try and save what little dignity he had left. Perhaps he could just tell them he was worried about what was to come, seeing as it was becoming a shorter and shorter distance till then.

The closer that they got to the border, the more Asman could feel the shift in the air. Niallen was no longer alone in his scenting of the air, as Asman had begun to smell it too.

The scent of death, just like in his nightmare, was thick and heady in the air. Sweet, but rotten at the same time and worrying to Asman as it became stronger while they traveled.

It seemed none of the other Guards noticed the stench besides Niallen, who would grimace occasionally. Asman did not like that he did not hate the smell. He knew it had to do with his magic; something changing in his mind to actually like the scent of decomposing corpses.

Perhaps it was to only make him more willing to kill, and this set Asman even more on edge while he sniffed the air casually.

The last night before the border left Asman in a haze of trying to spar with Niallen while also attempting to not focus on the scent, though the man was in the same situation. Niallen noticed Asman's distractions and gave up on sparring within the first few moments.

"You can smell it?" Niallen asked as he tossed his sword to the ground.

Asman sighed and nodded while also dropping his sword down to the ground, sitting down where he was standing in the small patch of a clearing they had found to train. It was a distance away from the others, since Niallen and him fought long after the Guard fell asleep.

Niallen sat down next to him with his own sigh, grimacing when he inhaled too harshly.

"We will get used to it, but for now it is diverting too much focus away." Niallen said and leaned back on his elbows, his legs coming to rest out in front of him.

Asman stared quietly in his own crisscrossed position, his back hunched over while he played with the grass.

"How can you smell things so well?" Asman asked, glancing back to his fingers as they idly killed single strands of grass.

"I have always been able to do so. My father said it was just something that happened to some people; nothing magic about it." Niallen shrugged easily.

Asman nodded again, but was silently surprised that the man had talked even a bit about his family. He had never done that before; at least not with Asman.

"Were you... are you close with him?" Asman inquired, forgetting that some people had parents that were alive still.

Niallen shifted slightly and pulled his elbows from the ground, letting his back lower to the ground. Asman tried not to stare at the mans lower regions as he was sure they were more pronounced through the thin trousers Niallen had on.

"We were. When I was a boy and would help him with the farmstead while my brothers were off. He died of illness a few years ago while I was in Gildren."

Asman no longer felt the need to stare at Niallen for his own selfish reasons, instead he looked to the mans face and frowned.

"I am sorry. I know how that feels, to lose a parent you were close to." Asman whispered, so desperately wanting to reach out and grab Niallen's hand, but instead only lying down next to him.

The view from the ground was better; the stars were bright and shining, with the moon no where to be seen.

"Thank you, but it was something we all knew was coming. My mother prepared us for the worst once he started to show more symptoms. It happened after my sister was killed, so we already knew how to deal with death." Niallen's tone being more somber than usual.

Asman frowned, remembering that Niallen's sister had died in battle. She had Shadow Magic, similar to his own Death Magic.

"Your sister, she fought for Isadren?" He asked, disliking how sad Niallen sounded, but appreciating that he would trust Asman with his story.

"Yes. Near the beginning of the war, in one of the first larger battles at the border. She led an army of nearly six hundred soldiers. Rasina was one of the only Shadow Mages to have a good control over her magic; but even then she had gotten too caught up in the fight." Niallen exhaled slowly and ran a hand over his face.

"I am sorry, we do not have to talk about this." Asman started up. Wanting to know more about him was not a good enough reason to put Niallen through any hardships.

"No, no, it is fine. I think she would have liked to be spoken about. My brothers rarely talk about her anymore, and my mother does not even think of her as to not resurface old memories. Rasina was... she was bright, and beautiful, and despite her magic she kept an open mind to the world." Niallen smiled slightly, his eyes lit from the far away fires of camp.

Asman smiled also, wondering what the woman would have looked like, how she spoke, how she held herself. He imagined her similar to Niallen.

"She had gotten married a few years before the battle; I was only twenty, but it is still one of my best memories with her. Her wife was from Felias, and had not had the best childhood, so when Cera came to Isadren and met Rasina, they fell in love almost immediately." Niallen grinned, but the upturned lips soon fell while speaking. "We do not talk to Cera that much anymore. I know my younger brother Desmond still visits her though."

"Does she live in the mountains too?"

"No, she moved to the Capital with Rasina while she led the troops. Cera just stayed there and became a blacksmith. Desmond spends the summer at the Capital for schooling before heading back home." Niallen's face luckily smoothed out a bit, with a more relaxed expression rather than sad.

"How old is Desmond? What does he study?" Asman questioned easily; perhaps the younger brother would be there when they arrived finally.

"He is coming into his twenty third winter now. I remember when he was just a babe, and when he got older lost all his childlike cuteness and became a tyrant." Niallen chuckled, straight smile showing his teeth and causing Asman to laugh too. "Last time I spoke to him he was studying to become a royal advisor on the queens court. He has always been intelligent when it came to politics."

"What about your other brother?"

"Rossnen is older than both me and Desmond, but younger than Rasina. He usually stays with my mother in the mountains; they both are tailors and it works well for him to watch over her as well. He is the eldest now, so he felt it was his responsibility to look after the farmstead when father died. My mother tried to convince him and his wife to move closer to the Capital, but both of them were content with staying."

"Do they have any children?"

"They should have two by now. Helnie was pregnant before I left, and their first born will be five soon." Niallen was smiling and yet again it turned slightly melancholic. "They named her Rasina. If this new babe is a boy, I imagine he would have my fathers name."

Asman hummed in understanding; Sam has the same idea for if he ever found someone to marry and have children with. Now, Asman could only help but think the same for his brother instead if he ever had children.

"Do you miss them?" Asman asked hesitantly and softly, the tiredness from the day was creeping onto him now.

Niallen stayed quiet for a moment, the sounds of the night filling the silence between them. Asman had desperately been trying to curb the annoyance at the chatter, and now he could proudly say that this moment was nice with the bugs and wildlife in the background.

"Yes, I do miss them. Everyday, when it comes to be too long of a journey. I... I cannot help but feel that sometimes I will not be able to come home to them. That I will die doing what I do." Niallen spoke softly. "But it is also something I feel I need to do, in order to bring peace in Calia. They understand that, but it still worries me. That I will be killed and leave one of the Guards to bring home that news to them."

Asman nodded, even though he was sure that Niallen was staring at the stars the same as him.

He could never imagine dying this far away from Sam, and having to have someone else tell him of his death. Asman figured that did not matter now, but metaphorically he could understand.

"Are you scared of death?" Asman asked with a whisper; this question perhaps could have been more related to him than what was apparent.

"No. I have never been frightened of things like that. Death is inevitable, and it comes for all of us whether or not you are lucky if it only comes when you are old. I have made peace with my gods and know when I die I will be welcomed by them. But... even then, it is the fear that the people still alive when I leave will be hurt that haunts me. The Guard would need a new leader, and there is always the possibility they will not be a good one. My family will feel my loss just the same as the ones previously." Niallen's voice and tone was enough to shake Asman to his core; he had never heard the man talk so fearfully. "It is only that which scares me. What happens to my loved ones once I pass on?"

Asman exhaled shakily, finally pushing aside his own fear and taking Niallen's hand in his.

"You said so yourself, death comes to us all. Some people might fight it, or not want to believe it has happened, but they will realize the truth soon enough. They might be hurt, or sad, or angry at death. It is only natural to want the people you love in your life; though there comes the time that they know they will not be alone after you are gone. It is the other people, who might even be grieving for you as well, that will help them keep your memory alive. The ones that will speak your name and tell your stories and make sure that even when you die, you are kept alive at the same time." Asman smiled gently, squeezing softly at Niallen's intertwined fingers. "It is all we can do to make sure there was a purpose for you living in the first place."

Niallen remained quiet after that, squeezing back as Asman's fingers eventually.

Asman could feel the way that his chest began to tingle, not unlike when he used his magic, but it was different this time.

It was still his magic, but not in the ways he had used it before. Rather, this time it was a more pleasant feeling, like wrapping up in a warm blanket on a cold day, or settling into a cool bath after you had been hot and sweaty.

The feeling went straight to his fingers and palm, spreading out and dispersing into Niallen's hand also. The only way Asman could tell the man could feel it was by the soft hum he let out.

It was not death, or pleasure, but it was comfort.

Comfort that was related to the peacefulness of knowing you are loved even when you die, and that love will not simply fall away once you are gone.

Chapter Sixteen: Storm

T he next day was the day that they finally reached the border.

The sky was cloudy, and the scent of both life and death was hanging in the air, testing Asman's ability to distinguish the two.

He could tell that they were coming to the place where a battle had been fought. With the scent of dead bodies and blood it was almost obvious. But there was also the light scent of men, fires, and mud.

It made sense for there to be a fort at the border. It would leave the possibility of either side gaining ground at a standstill.

The Isadrenians could not pass the fort without conquering it, and the Feliasians could not go further beyond the Isadrenian fort either.

The road that the Guard had been on would unfortunately lead right to Fort Jasdan, named after the river that separated the two kingdoms; and even though the fort was likely near empty, the Guard would not take it over until they knew that they could defeat the line of Feliasian soldiers across the river.

In the letter, it read that Fort Aidell of Isadren had not yet been invaded, but was on the brink of it.

Niallen, Stulvon, Asman, and Vanora has all been the ones to speak of a plan. Vanora was one of the best strategists in the Guard, Stulvon was Niallen's second, and since Asman had called them to fight technically, those were the ones that Niallen chose to speak with.

Since the forts and the bridge to cross the river were at the thinnest part of the river, it would take the Guard traveling through the forest to get to another spot that they could cross at. Even though it was one of the widest areas in the river, the place where they would cross held two small islets within the water. This would give them enough shallow spaces to be able to walk or at least swim the horses across.

Once they were across, there would be a short walk to the north gate at Fort Aidell. Asman quickly realized that it would be easy for the Guard to just continue north on the road towards the Capital, yet when he mentioned this, Niallen and the other two had been quick to say that they were willing to fight still.

If the Feliasian numbers were still too great, then they could just as easily return to the Capital and send more men with a more accurate account of their numbers.

After telling the Guard the plan, that is what left them now quickly approaching the Jasdan river and its islets.

The walk through the forest had to be quiet, just in case there were soldiers hunting or patrolling the nearby wood. The Guard stayed on their horses just in case they would need to run, and for the sound of only at most the horses hoofbeats and not human footsteps.

They were far enough from the fort that they could not see the walls, but close enough that once they reached the river, it was easy to see the bridge not too far down from them.

In addition to the bridge, were also the two clearings which were used for battle. One held the smell of death that had been bothering Niallen and Asman, and one held the smell of life and the soldiers they meant to avoid and then attack.

The river was large, but the islets truly did provide shallow water. Shallow, but also not so enough that the Guard could walk across. So then they went through the motions of gathering the bags and stripping what clothes they could as to not get them wet.

The larger horses went first, with the tallest Guards guiding them as dry items were held above their heads; Niallen and Stulvon were in this group along with Cedran.

Asman was cold without the shirt and trousers he had stripped of, and all of the shorter Guards were the same as him. Dahlia stood next to him as they led themselves into the frigid river next.

Despite being a fair distance from the river, it was still imperative to keep quiet, which was why Asman covered his mouth while he gasped at the cold water.

The horses had little to no issue crossing to each small patch of trees in the river, and besides a few snorts of displeasure they were as quiet as the Guard.

When they finally stepped onto the other side of the river, Asman gladly took his clothes and horse back from Cheden, who grinned smugly at both him and Dahlias shivering and half naked forms.

While the Guard replaced their wet undergarments with dry tunics and trousers, the horses were stripped of their own saddles and tack in order to let them fully dry. They of course tried to dry them off as best they could with a couple blankets before leaving them be.

Small fires were made and wet clothes were hung to dry. Asman huddled under his dry cloak and a blanket from his bedroll next to the fire. Dahlia and Teran pressed up against him in attempts to find more warmth, and Asman could not care in the slightest as he tried to do the same.

They only stayed at the river banks long enough to regain at least some body temperature back before packing back up and heading back east to Fort Aidell.

This time, they kept the horses tack off and in their arms as the Guard walked the horses, hoping the exercise would help them some.

It did help, and by nightfall, they were staring down the northern gate of the Isadrenian fort. Asman watching as Niallen carefully spoke to the guards standing at said gate.

Once they were made aware of who the Guard actually were, the gates were opened with haste and allowed the shivering men, women, and others in.

Asman had been expecting the worse before they entered, but it could not have prepared him for what he actually saw.

The fort had a few buildings in it, though most of the soldiers were outside. All of them either laying on the ground wounded or helping those who were the former.

Niallen immediately ordered for the Guard to help with the injured, while he himself quickly walked off to the main and largest
building.

The horses were led to a pen with water and food, and the Guard
did as they were told. Each one rushing off to help with the carnage
laid across the dirt packed ground.

Asman himself did not think twice before going to those who
seemed they would not make it. Those with wounds that were too
great for the victim to survive.

The first he came across was a man, his stomach and innards exposed while a soldier tried to wipe sweat from his brow and had a
drastic look on his face.

"Hello." Asman greeted softly, kneeling down on one side of the
man. "I would like to help if that is alright?"

The man blearily looked up at him, as well as the soldier, who was
looking at him as if he was insane.

"Ya cannot help me, Kid. There are others who need it more than
I." He rasped out, shaking his head as well as he could while it was
laid in the soldiers lap.

The dying man was older, with gray and brown hair cropped short
and matted with sweat.

"I think I could though, if you allowed me? My name is Asman.
What is yours, sir?" Asman asked gently, keeping his hands in his lap
while he waited for an answer.

"Gossor." The man replied, a sharp intake making his face scrunch in pain. "How could you help me? You got something that will take the pain away?"

Asman frowned and exhaled shakily, his eyes shooting back and forth from the grotesque wound to Gossor's face.

"Perhaps. I... I have Death Magic, sir. If you would allow it, I could help to make your death less painful. You must know that there is nothing anyone can do for you now that will allow you to live, but there are better ways to die than bleeding out or succumbing to fever." Asman sighed, now keeping his eyes on Gossor to test the mans reaction.

The mans perpetual frown seemed to deepened and he closed his eyes with a shaky sigh.

"I do not care what you do, Kid. I always knew I was destined to die in battle. I only... I want me sword in my hand while I die." Gossor moved one of the hands at his side to face palm up.

The soldier under him gave a sad look, but reached for the sword nearby anyway, placing it in Gossor's hand. The dying man tightened his grip and inhaled deeply and nodded to Asman.

Asman slowly reached out a hand to place it against the mans bare chest, wiry hairs tickling and warm against his palm. The soldier made a noise and grasped at Gossor's free hand, giving some contact to the dying man.

It was not hard to find his magic, and once Asman did, he slowly let the tingling from his own chest travel to Gossor's. The magic he first let go was meant to soothe him, to make death seem smoother and to make the flame within Gossor calm to the point that Asman could carefully dim it.

Gossor did not react once Asman started to dwindle the light away, he only sighed and went lax, the pain easing until it was gone.

The heart beating against Asman's palm slowed and slowed and slowed, until it was altogether gone. The light gone in a silent glow and a final breath.

Asman stayed there for a moment, taking in the now dead man in front of him. The soldier had his head tipped down, a single tear rolling down dirty cheeks.

Eventually, Asman took his hand from Gossor's chest, the sounds of the fort finally coming back to his ears while he refocused on his surroundings.

"Will you be okay?" Asman asked the soldier quietly.

"Y-yes. He just... he was a good friend." The soldier muttered and wiped the stray tear away, looking back up at Asman with red eyes.

"I am sorry. He did a good thing, and even though he is gone, I am sure he is being rewarded by the gods for his sacrifice." Asman smiled softly standing slowly and patting the mans shoulder.

The soldier nodded and inhaled deeply.

"Thank you, Asman."

Asman nodded slightly, walking off when the man looked back down to his fallen friend.

There were many more soldiers in the same situation as Gossor, it was as if Asman was drawn to them and could tell who of them were closer to their deaths.

Each time, he sat down, told them his name and asked for theirs before letting them die in peace.

Each time, he watched and felt their light die underneath his hand, and each time, his mind cleared of all else going on around him.

By the twentieth man, Asman was walking up to those who already knew his name and were ready to die by his hands.

Some refused his help, but still thanked him for helping their friends, their brothers and sisters who fought by their side, have a calming death after the battle they had lost.

The Guard who were helping the injured caught on quickly to what Asman was doing and some would call him over to do so with the soldier they were with.

The moon was high above them by the time all those who wanted to die were dead. The heavily injured were sleeping with their wounds tended to, and the less injured were doing the same.

Dahlia noticed how tired Asman was when they finished and stole him away to one of the buildings to rest.

Niallen and most of the Guard were in the simple barracks also, around thirty cots spaced equally apart with a cooking fire in the middle. Most of the beds were pushed into a circle as seating around the fire, and there were bowls of stew in the Guards hands that made Asman realize just how hungry he was.

Asman sat down silently next to Niallen and toon the bowl of food when offered, eating just as quietly as the rest of the Guard. They had seen something terrible here, and Asman doubted there would be any laughter or joking tonight.

The cots that were not previously around the fire were pushed so that they were, making the singular ones double in size enough for two people to sleep.

Asman sensed that no one wanted to sleep alone tonight, and he was alright with that, he did not really want to either.

One by one, the Guard turned in and laid down, filling the air with snores and leaving Asman still sitting while staring at the fire.

He was tired, but he did not want to sleep yet. There was too much on his mind.

The people he helped die had families, and each had their owns lives, but now they were gone. The war had provided them fatal wounds and ripped them from the world without hesitation.

Would some of the Guard die once they fought against the Feliasian soldiers? Would Asman need to help them die also? Would he do what he had been denying since finding his magic and kill his friends?

"Asman, are you alright?" Niallen's voice interrupted his thoughts quietly, careful not to wake all the other Guards who were sleeping.

"No, but if I was that would be more worrying." Asman sighed and shut his eyes, sniffing and running a hand through his hair.

"You helped a lot of people tonight. They would have had painful and slow deaths without you." Niallen stated from beside him.

"I know. But it does not make me feel any better." Asman opened his eyes again and huffed. "Thirty-seven men and women. That is how many I killed tonight. I cannot help but think that after this

battle, there might be Guards that I have to do the same for, and I...
I still was the one wanted them to fight with me."

"You did not kill those soldiers, Asman. Felias did. There is always
risk of people dying during a war, but what you did, or will do, was
never killing. You might want them to fight with you, but they feel
the same way. These people want to go to battle with you as much
as you them. You gave them a choice and that is all you can do,
you cannot change the outcome regardless of hard you try." Niallen
whispered with a frown.

Asman only nodded slightly and sniffed again, snuffing out the
urge to cry. He was so sick of crying all the time.

Without any more words, Asman pulled off his boots and pulled
his legs up onto the cot. He pushed off onto the other side and the
other cot, lying down with his back to both the fire and Niallen.

He felt Niallen do the same and in a moment there was the warmth
of another body radiating closer to Asman's.

Asman could not even muster the energy to care that he was in one
way sleeping with Niallen.

He only curled up under his blanket and let himself drift off after
an eventful day.

Chapter Seventeen: Blood

Unfortunately, it only took until just before dawn for the Guard to be woken by yelling and footsteps running.

Asman snapped awake just as the rest of them did, his eyes burning from the lack of sleep, but aware that he needed to get out of bed and help with whatever caused the noise.

Quickly, he joined the rest of the Guard, snatching up his sword and armor and hastily slipping it on. Asman followed Niallen while buckling the few straps at his side and stepping outside with his sword in hand.

Half of the forts occupants were running towards the southern gate, as the rest rushed to wake anyone who was still sleeping.

Asman and the Guard followed Niallen quickly, the man with his own sword out while attempting to find the captain of the the fort. The fort being in such a state of chaos, it was hard to fine the woman in charge.

"Commander!" Niallen finally yelled once said woman was in his sights. "What is happening?"

The Commander looked to Niallen swiftly while she stayed at a steady and fast pace to the gate, her dirty face framed by bright red hair. She had a worried look that quickly transferred over to Asman's.

Had the Feliasian soldiers begun to attack? There was yelling from both sides of the fort walls, so had they possibly found a way over them?

"The Feliasians are shooting arrows over the wall, some of them aflame and some not. They still have not breached the walls or gate, but if we do not do something then it will only be a matter of time." The Commander gritted out, finally making it a place where Asman could see the arrows arching over the walls. "They are antagonizing us because they know we are small in number."

Niallen took in the information the same as Asman, the former clenching his jaw and swiftly dodging a single arrow that had come too close.

"We need to get everyone inside or against the walls while I think." Niallen ordered both the Commander and the Guard.

Both nodded and Asman watched as they set to gathering the soldiers with the new directive. Asman stayed and followed Niallen as they pressed up against the stone fort wall.

"Niallen-"

"No. I know that you likely have some irrational idea going on in your head that will likely end in you dying, so no, Asman." Niallen bit out and kept to the wall while he walked towards the southern gate.

"You do not know what I was going to say! It is a perfectly rational plan and only would result in my death if I was thick." Asman huffed and glared at Niallen's back, the man slowing while they got closer to the large wooden door.

Niallen easily turned to give Asman a look that very clearly showed what he thought about Asman not being thick.

"God, you are an arse, would you just listen to it before you turn it down? Unless you can think of another and better one while the Feliasians are shooting arrows over the fort walls?" Asman hissed at the man, who had returned to his creeping along the wall.

"Yes, in fact. We find out how many men there are and then attack." Niallen stopped as they reached the last few steps away from the gate.

"How do you expect to find out how many men there are? Are you going to open the gate and look?" Asman asked sarcastically with raised eyebrows even though Niallen could not see him.

Asman waited for a few moments for an answer before scoffing and resisting the urge to smack Niallen on the back of his head.

"Look, my plan needs darkness to work, and seeing as the sun will likely be rising soon, you either need to make a decision or I am leaving without your permission." Asman growled out at Niallen's back, which was still facing him.

"What do you think you are going to do, Asman? Run out there and just count? They will see you in a second and kill you regardless if you say your a Feliasian or not." Niallen whipped around to finally face Asman, his face contorted in irritation.

"No, you idiot, I am going to tell the truth." Asman contorted his own face to match the mans. "I was a prisoner and the Guard captured me after my village was attacked, I got free during the chaos and ran while you were all distracted. I figure out how many soldiers there are and sneak away back here."

"What if they do not believe you and kill you even after you say your part? Better yet, what if they kill you before you even speak? Asman, there are too many unknown variables for a plan like that to work."

"They will not kill me. I look Feliasian, I sound Feliasian, I can tear up a tunic and smear dirt on my face and they will be none the wiser. There is no way that these soldiers could have heard about Thamor already, so it will be easy to say that the Guard were the ones to burn it. You took me as a trophy, to show the queen that you succeeded in destroying a village." Asman waved his sword free hand around convincingly.

Niallen exhaled deeply through his nose and ran a hand over his mouth, thinking about what Asman had told him.

"You are sure you can convince them of that?" Niallen looked briefly down at Asman, who grinned and nodded.

"I convinced Sam I liked women for twenty six years. Trust me when I say that I can do this Niallen." Asman flashed a more serious look to the man.

Niallen sighed and glanced around, his jaw clenching when another arrow was shot down into the dirt a short distance away.

"Fine. Though I swear to the gods if you are not back by nightfall, at the latest, then I will... I will sell Cedran." Niallen glared without any real anger towards Asman.

Asman snorted and smirked, but the small smile soon dropped as he thought of some other things.

"Niallen, in all seriousness, if I do not come back... make sure Thamor gets its justice, alright? Make sure that Sam and I did not die for nothing." Asman grimaced a tight look off to the side, his hand gripping and releasing on the handle of his sword.

Niallen frowned, but nodded firmly anyway.

That was that then. Asman would infiltrate the group of Feliasian soldiers and on a off chance, perhaps die.

———————

Asman sprinted through the forest and towards the light of the Feliasian campfires, the fort wall to his left while the trees whipped past him.

He had torn his shirt as much as he could in such a short span of time, along with ripping holes in the knees of his trousers and scrubbing dry dirt through his hair. His heart was pounding as he got closer to the camp.

The final distance before stepping into the clearing, he made sure to frantically look behind him and put on a terrified look.

Asman tore through into the clearing quickly, sprinting up to the group of maybe forty soldiers sitting around a fire; the rest of the fleet was likely at the walls still shooting arrows.

"Oh, thank god. I-I got out! T-They had me prisoner, and-and with the arrows and no one was looking and I got out!" Asman sputtered, heaving greedy breaths as he skidded to a Stop right in front of the soldiers.

They all stood up and some even took out their swords; smart, but not what Asman wanted.

"What the fuck? Who the hell are you, Kid?" One of the soldiers asked, his sword pointed threateningly at Asman's throat.

"Please, please, I-I... My name is Asman. I am from Thamor. The-The Isa- Those heathens destroyed it and they took me! They were going to bring me the Queen as a t-trophy, but the attack! You, you guys saved me!" Asman held up his hands pathetically, his face still marred with fear, but a fake look of relief also.

The soldiers all looked at both Asman and the others warily, processing what he had said. Asman shivered unwillingly against the cold wind through his tunic, almost glad that it added to his poor defenseless look.

"What makes you think we believe this? We should kill you and just be done with it." Another soldier stated with bared teeth, yet another sword tip against Asman's throat.

"No! No, I can... I can tell you about them! I know how many soldiers are in the fort, and, and the group that took me I can tell you about them too." Asman stared with wide eyes flickering back and forth between the two soldiers, not wanting to look at the others and show any more braveness than need be.

The soldiers gave another wary look between themselves and also the tree line that just beyond held the fort.

Asman panted quickly, his heart still racing while the men in front of him decided whether or not he would live.

"You can stay breathing for now, but you have to tell us all you know." What seemed like the main soldier stated and dropped his sword from Asman's neck, causing the other to do the same.

Asman let out a relieved breath and slowly lowered his hands, nodded fervently while the soldier pointed to a seat next to the fire. Asman swiftly sat down and tried to regain some warmth.

"How many men do they have?" The soldier asked immediately and sat down also. The rest of the group did so too after him and continued to stare at Asman.

"Fifty, at most." Asman lied easily. "The group I was with only had a dozen, and the fort was mostly only full of injured and dying."

In truth, there were nearly seventy soldiers including the Guard that could fight without issue. Asman still had no idea how many Feliasians there actually were, but allowing them to think they had a better advantage would help in the long run.

The soldier seemed to believe the lie and laughed heartily, some of the other soldiers joining him in smirks and chuckles.

"We should have known those barbarians would retreat to their fort when their numbers became small. With how many men we have we could easily invade through the gate and take the fort." The soldier waved a hand around as if he had told a joke. "The cowards could not even put up a fight."

Asman withheld his anger with a bitten tongue. Isadrenians were not barbarians or cowards, they were anything but that.

The soldier began to say something more, but was interrupted by a large group filing into the clearing; the rest of the Feliasians had returned.

The men were laughing and smacking each other on the backs, speaking loudly of how they hoped they got some good hits in.

Asman heatedly ignored the comments and set to work on counting how many soldiers there actually were.

In addition to the forty men around the fire, around sixty returned from the gates, making just over one hundred Feliasian soldiers in Isadren territory.

Asman hid the irritated thoughts he had. Even though there were seventy Isadrenians, they would still be overmatched by the extra thirty from Felias. He had told Niallen that all he would do was count, but there was a need in the pit of his stomach to do something more; to try and cut the numbers some.

There was little he could do without being caught and killed. The soldiers were everywhere in the clearing, and the sun was rising quickly to the east over the forest.

Though, there were soldiers walking off in the woods to relieve themselves... if he could perhaps ask to piss, kill the soldier that came with him, because there was little chance they would send him alone, and then kill whatever soldiers came to check when they took too long. That could work. Then when he had killed enough of them, he could quickly run back to the fort.

Asman glanced around and found that nearly all the soldier that had been looking at him were now greeting the others from the fire. No one had their eyes on him, except for the soldier beside him; the second one that held a sword to his throat.

"Can-Can I go piss?" Asman asked quietly to the man, submissive eyes trying to guilt the soldier.

"I suppose that would be fine. Come on." The soldier sighed and stood, a hand to the handle of his sword that was back in its sheath across his hip. "I am taking the kid to go piss, should be back in a moment."

Asman stood slowly while the soldier announce this to the rest of the fire, watching while they nodded their heads offhandedly before returning to their conversations.

He let himself be guided to the forest line to the west, the closest to the fire, but also only a short distance from where Asman had come from.

The soldier stopped him just out of eyesight of the others, a few thick trees hiding them from the clearing.

Asman did not waist time in finding his magic, though instead of letting it reach his fingers, he let it go through his shoulder, where the soldiers hand was placed threateningly.

Without another word, the man dropped to the forest floor with a thud and Asman sighed in relief.

"Serves you right, you fuck." Asman muttered and leaned down to begin pulling the soldiers dead body away from the path and behind a tree.

He climbed in said tree and waited for a while until another soldier came looking for them.

This time Asman leaped down and jumped onto the soldiers back, not using his magic but instead just the crook of his elbow to steal the breath away from the man.

Again, Asman climbed into the tree after hiding the body. Each time another soldier came, or sometimes two or three or even four, Asman would come down from where he was hiding and kill the men.

He hardly ever used his magic, but he was still strong without it; the men still ended up dead either way.

Asman, by the time there were at least twenty men stacked in a pile, was huffing and panting and hating what he had done. The feeling of killing them was not the problem, in fact, it was the feeling that made it so easy to keep doing it. It was instead the nagging feeling that these men had no clue what they were doing that was causing Asman's chest to clench uncomfortably.

The soldiers likely did not know that Felias was corrupt, or that their brethren had murdered villages that could have even been theres at some point. They did not know that the people whom they were fighting were human beings just like them, and were not what King Osetren had told them they were.

While staring at the pile of men, Asman inhaled sharply and shook away the tears.

These men also could have had families, and were fighting just for them in fear that the war could take them away. They could have had brothers and sisters and parents and children and wives, but Asman killed them without mercy.

Asman exhaled deeply and steeled himself; there was only so much time before the rest of the soldiers would realize what was actually happening and send too many men for Asman to handle. The sounds of another group of men were already getting closer, so with another remorseful look to the dead men, Asman began jogging back towards the fort walls.

Once he was far enough away from both the clearing and his kill site, Asman slowed down and walked the rest of the way to the northern gate.

There were a few cuts and bruises throbbing on various parts of his body, the one slice on his cheek stinging from the tears that had started without Asman's knowledge.

Figuring that he would not get out of shedding the tears, Asman have in and softly cried while he walked, the fort wall to his right as he curved around to the gate.

The soldiers guarding the entrance immediately caught sight of his solemn figure and wordlessly opened the gate enough for Asman to slide through, the latter wiping the tears and fresh blood from his face as best he could.

The fort was again bustling while the soldiers and occasionally a Guard would pass by with pales of water or sacks of food. The Guard who saw Asman would greet him kindly, but there were no smiles while they took in the way he looked.

Asman did his best to greet them back on his walk towards the main building, where he was sure Niallen and the Commander were speaking battle strategies.

Though, before he could reach the building, he was being crushed in a hug by Dahlia the moment she saw him.

"Oh gods, Asman I was so worried! It seems I had good reason too, look at you, you are covered in wounds!" Dahlia exclaimed and pulled back so that she could stress the numerous cuts at his skin.

"Dahlia, as much as I would appreciate your time, I am afraid I have information for Niallen and the Commander." Asman smiled softly and set his hands at her shoulders; his head just above hers while they stood in front of each other.

"Right. Right, that is probably best. I will come with you." Dahlia exhaled shakily and grabbed for Asman's arm, pulling quickly back towards the building.

Asman huffed shortly and let her do so, the two of them reaching it in no time with Dahlias insistent rushing.

The main building only had one level and one room, but that one room was larger than the rest of the smaller barracks and storehouses within the fort. This is why when the door opened and both Asman and Dahlia entered, the former was left looking into Niallen's surprised face.

"Asman." He let out with a sigh of relief.

"Niallen. I have the numbers for the Feliasians."

Chapter Eighteen:
Battle

Asman froze when a set of rather large arms encircled his shoulders, Niallen's breath hitting the back of his neck.

"I am glad you made it back safely, Asman." Niallen said softly and pulled back before Asman could even think to return the hug.

"I was only gone for half of the day." Asman muttered while his cheeks flushed, the feeling of Niallen's arms still lingering in tingles on his skin.

"Still, I was worried they would kill you. Even though I see you are not unharmed, you are not dead and that is excellent." Niallen grimaced and pointed to the red cut on Asman's face.

"Y-yes... right, uh, the soldiers." Asman stammered slightly, finally breaking the intense eye contact with Niallen in order to look at the Commander also. "The have just over eighty of them now."

"Now? What do you mean by that?" The Commanders brows furrowed together and Asman stepped carefully out from in front of Niallen, coming to stand closer to the woman he was speaking to.

"There were one hundred previously. I realized that it may be easier to battle on more even grounds, so I leveled them more." Asman clasped his hands in front of him. "I wish I could have done more, but the groups were getting larger once they caught on to what was happening."

"What did happen, Asman?" Niallen asked incredulously and walked forward enough so that he was practically standing next to the Commander.

"I pretended to have to piss and then killed whatever soldiers came to find me after a while." Asman plainly stated as he withheld the emotions swirling in his mind in favor of looking put together. "Again, I only was able to kill twenty before they caught on."

Niallen inhaled deeply and shook his head disapprovingly. Though, the Commander still seemed to be processing.

"Asman, you were only supposed to count their numbers, not kill them." Niallen sighed out with a glare, which as always, made Asman glare right back at him.

"It was not as if it was hard. You know how I feel about this; if there was any chance to better this fight so that we could win then I was going to take it, Niallen." Asman scoffed at the man, his composure breaking slightly.

Dahlia was still standing quietly behind them, but she took that moment to exit back through the door. Asman knew she would talk to him after he was done.

"Still, we could have handled only a hundred men. What you did only resulted in more injuries that were unnecessary." Niallen growled out and crossed his arms, the leather from his armor creaking slightly.

"Oh no, I hope the women do not think I am ugly now." Asman spat back with a false worried look, causing Niallen to huff and open his mouth.

Though, the moment the man began to talk, he was interrupted by the Commander.

"You killed twenty men? On your own? I was under the impression that you just began training a fortnight ago." She said with her hands splayed across the thick wooden desk in front of her.

Asman exhaled slowly and looked back to the Commander, ignoring Niallen in favor of showing the woman some respect.

"Yes, ma'am. Niallen has been training me. Though, the soldiers did not know that, and I had the element of surprise against them."

"Twenty men is still a good amount, especially as soldiers. You are lucky you only came out with a few cuts and bruises. I also know you have Death Magic, am I correct to assume you used that on some of them?" The Commander questioned and Asman shifted slightly.

"For the first soldier, yes. But, the... the rest I did not." Asman glanced to the cobblestone floor briefly before looking back to the Commander, not wanting to seem disrespectful if he looked away for too long.

"You must learn fast then, to be able take down as many men after just two weeks of training." The Commander raised eyebrows and sent a look to Niallen, who seemed to puff up at the praise.

"Thank you, ma'am." Asman flushed once more, not knowing what else to say to something like that.

Praise from Niallen was something nice, and Asman liked it, but praise from someone who did not know him and still thought he did well was different and welcomed.

"Anyway, we should prepare to launch the attack. The more time we wait, the more time we give the Feliasians time for more of them to come. Do they know how many of us there are, Asman?" The Commander asked as she switched back over to being the one in charge.

"I told them that there are only fifty able to fight. They believed me then, but now that they know I was no who I said I was they might think differently." Asman stated with a slight shake of his head.

"But they are uncertain either way and that will benefit us. If we attack now, they will still be scrambling from the lose of twenty men." Niallen piped in, directing his words to the Commander, who was nodding her head in agreement.

"Check with the injured and see if there are some who can fight. I will work on gathering the soldiers near the southern gate." The Commander ordered easily and came out from behind her desk. "Asman, get your amor and sword, your help will be needed too."

Asman nodded and rushed to follow Niallen, who was already heading for the door back out into the fort.

While Niallen went towards the barracks filled with the injured, Asman quickly walked back to the Guards barracks and snatched up his amor in sword that had been placed there for safekeeping.

He stripped the torn tunic and trousers to replace them with his own; the ones he had ripped were a spare pair that could have been from a dead soldier. Asman tried to wipe as much dirt from his face as possible after wetting the torn tunic with some spit and scrubbing at his cheeks, careful around the cut that was scabbing over still.

The other cuts on his arms were wrapped with small strips of the tunic so that at the very least they did not get dirt in them while fighting.

Once he finished, Asman made sure to buckle his armor back in place and fasten his sword around his waist before sprinting back out to join the small army forming at the gate.

The sun was a bit past noon, but it barely showed through the wispy clouds forming. Asman could see that some thicker and perhaps thunder clouds were blowing in from the north; there was a good chance that it would rain the coming night.

The Commander and Niallen had both done their jobs and gathered those who would fight in the gap of space right in front of the southern gate.

Asman filed through the decent number of soldiers to find the Guard, who were standing just as ready as the rest. He found Dahlia and Teran near the front, with Niallen just ahead of them next to Stulvon.

The Commander was at the very head of the group, already speaking and giving the soldiers a speech about why they were doing this.

Asman listened to her give thanks to those who had died in battle for their sacrifice, and pray that if they should do so also, may they die with their sword in hand and a Feliasian soldier dead beneath them.

The small army cheered war cried after she finished, but Asman kept his lips sealed and his fist lowered. He could feel that someone was going to die.

Whether it was only the soldier beside him, or one of the Guard, he could feel that they would not survive the coming battle.

Though, it was just that, a battle. People would die and Asman knew this. Would more soldiers had died if they did not come? Was asking the Guard to fight actually something that could save lives? Even if some could die in the end?

Asman was pulled from his thoughts by the gates opening, the battalion moving forward and out onto the short road that led to the clearing.

It did not take long for the Feliasians to realize what was happening near the northern part of the clearing, as Isadrenian soldiers swarmed out and began fighting immediately.

In an instant, the two sides were fighting and the sounds of swords clashing was filling the air, yells of pain or shouts of war came at Asman. The speed of it all shocked Asman while also seeming like it was normal. It definitely was not was he had imagined though; the Guard flying into action and charging at Feliasian men with no hesitation.

He himself had to wait a moment for a Feliasian soldier to find him, but once he did, they easily met with swords.

The Feliasians had leather armor same as the Isadrenians, but theres was died black, and had more metal embellishments than the simple brown Asman and the others were wearing.

This is why it was so easy to slide his sword in the Feliasians chest; the leather could help against cuts, but not the point and power behind a stab.

After that, the next Feliasian to find him died just the same, and after that, Asman worked on helping those soldiers who seemed to be stuck in a fight with no real winning side. He would come up behind the Feliasian and run his sword through them before giving a nod and moving on.

The battle so far seemed to be favoring the Isadrenians; the Feliasians had been thankfully surprised by the attack, but there were still those who fought well and were easy to fall into the motions of war.

Asman, while fighting his way through the field, checked each body that fell. Most were Feliasians, but there were still a fair amount of Isadrenians. It was only when he came across a familiar face that he paused and ran to them.

Hamen was breathing shallowly, shaking hand pressed against a large bleeding wound in his stomach. He back on the ground and his face up towards the sky, Asman skidded down next to him on his knees.

"Hamen!" Asman yelled and looked wildly into the older mans eyes, which seemed relieved for Asman to be there.

"Azzy. G-glad you are here, boy. My-My sword fell, and it is just out of reach. Y-you know we cannot die without our swords." Hamen grunted and pointed towards his sword, a bloody smirk twitching at his lips.

Asman inhaled sharply and withheld tears, instead reaching for the sword and quickly placing the leather wrapped handle in Hamens hand.

"Thank you. I-I guess I should say my goodbyes then?" Hamen chuckled but grimaced when it jostled his stomach. "Listen, Azzy. Y-You are doing good as a Guard. We were all surprised when Niallen chose you, but after seeing what you can do? It was clear that he made the right choice."

Asman clenched his eyes shut and nodded, the tears stinging painfully.

"I am old, and ready to go to Grethen. I do not have any family besides the Guard, so we are lucky it was me and not Vanora or Nyana. I am glad I will die in battle, but I do not want to die from blood lose, Azzy." Hamen looked at Asman with a telling look.

"You want me t-to?" Asman stuttered out and sniffed; both Hamen and him knew what he was asking.

"You have a good handle on your magic. I trust you to keep that up, and I swear if you go mad after this then I will be the only voice you hear." Hamen had a smile, but his voice was stern. Asman chuckled breathlessly and nodded, holding a shaky hand out to hover just above Hamens chest.

Asman looked back to Hamen, who nodded and shut his eyes with a sigh. Asman slowly lowered his hand and went to work at finding his magic.

He did his best to draw the pain away before finding Hamens light. With a final sniff and a single tear, Asman did as asked and took away Hamens suffering.

The sounds of the battle came back to his ears quickly and Asman knew that he should not stay near Hamen for too long. He took one last glance of where his body was before grabbing his sword and turning back to the fight.

The soldiers that remained were the strongest; the ones that had survived the weaker attacks and were now fighter stronger rivals.

Asman did his best to help where he could. His sword was dripping with blood, the steel stained with red, each stab or slice at another was sending someone else's blood into their wounds.

A singular Feliasian caught his eye after a moment, the man just finishing in killing an Isadrenian and who was now stalking towards another.

Asman gritted his teeth and jumped out in front of the soldier, holding his sword up as to ask the man for a fight.

The soldier growled and returned the stance, quickly striking out at Asman without waiting.

Asman cursed and dodged, circling around slowly as the soldier did so also. It was just like sparring with Niallen, only this time Asman's opponent actually wanted him dead and he returned that feeling.

He tried to strike, but the soldier dodged also, sending back his own stab at Asman that the latter slapped away with his sword.

Each strike, stab, clash, or drive was parried by either the soldier or Asman. Neither on had gotten a good hit in, and Asman was becoming irritated.

Asman had not noticed that his magic had flared up unknowingly, so he continued to dodge another attack from the soldier. It was not until the sword in his hand began getting darker in color that he quickly glanced at it and realized what was happening.

Black was spreading from the handle up to the tip, his magic flowing through the blade until every spot on the sword was pitch black, the blood on it deepening in color also.

The soldier looked to the sword in horror and then to Asman's face. Asman did not waste the distraction before shooting forward and slicing through the air towards the soldiers neck.

Unfortunately, the soldier dodged before Asman could land a fatal blow, but not enough so that the blackened sword did not nick his neck. Asman stared at the soldier, who had hissed and then unceremoniously dropped to the ground.

So, Asman had put some magic into his sword. Enough magic that it only took a small cut for the soldier to die almost instantaneously.

Not wanting to let his guard down just from the strange incident, Asman turned around and glanced at the field.

The battle was still occurring, but there were a lot less soldiers than before, allowing Asman to spot where most of the Guard was, including Niallen.

The man was fighting one on one with a soldier, and when Asman looked closer, he found that the soldier was the same one from earlier that had first threatened him and then allowed him to stay. It seemed Asman was right in assuming he was the main soldier or leader, seeing as how well he fought Niallen.

Asman could see that despite Niallen being an excellent fighter, the main soldier it seemed was fighting dirty; trying to kick and grab, attempting to trip Niallen or bend down to throw dirt. Asman glared at the childish act and began walking towards them.

The rest of the Guard and Isadrenians were doing a fine job of finishing off the Feliasians; it seemed they would be winning after all.

Though, even if they seemed to be winning, the soldier fighting Niallen did not get that fact and continued to try and stab at the latter.

It was only after the soldier managed to get a fistful if dirt and throw it in Niallen's eyes that he finally managed to get a good strike in, his sword sinking into Niallen's side with a sickening sound.

Asman froze and his eyes widened in horror. Niallen fell to the ground and clutched the wound, the blood seeping through his fingers and onto the ground, filling Asman with enough dread to make his heart beat stop.

The soldier smiled and backed away, purposely kicking a Niallen's sword out of his grip and reaching distance. This is what made Asman snap out of his mind.

He ran forward at full speed, colliding with the soldier with a thud as they both fell to the ground, Asman not pausing before lifting his sword and stabbing it down through the soldiers heart. Though, he did not stop even after the man was dead, only lifting the sword and stabbing repeatedly, until the body's chest was nothing but mangled blood, skin, and bone.

"Asman. Enough."

Asman growled and kept going, standing up over the body so that he could slash at the remains, his anger flowing through him and down the sword. If there was magic in it, there was no way to tell through the mess of blood and matter.

"Asman!"

Niallen's voice was sharp yet breathy, obviously taking a bit out of him with the wound in his side.

Asman froze once more and turned back to Niallen, remembering what had happened to the man before dropping his sword and rushing to him.

"Niallen. Fuck, fuck, fuck, what do I do?" Asman kneeled next to him quickly, holding his hands up as if he wanted to touch, but he did not know what to do.

"I will be fine, I just need to stop the bleeding." Niallen huffed out and grimaced, his hand still pressed hard into the wound.

Asman panted harshly, nodding before moving to undo the straps on his own armor. He quickly shucked it and his shirt off, tearing into the cloth with his teeth in order to strip off a piece.

"Right, um, c-can you lift up a little bit? S-so I can get this under the other side and get your armor off?" Asman asked shakily and wadded the cloth, hoping that if he at least had something to stop the bleeding on Niallen's back, then the front would be easier to do.

"No." Niallen gritted out after attempting to lift himself, his glare not towards Asman this time, but instead the sky that was darkening by the moment.

"Okay, okay that is fine. I can do it. Just- it will hurt, alright?" Asman placed a hand on Niallen's arm, gripping slightly.

"Just do it, Asman." Niallen bit out, before clenching his jaw again.

Asman frowned and used both hands to carefully undo the straps on the mans armor, pulling it off his arms and the wound before pushing Niallen up, wincing at the grunt the man let out while he settled the wad of cloth on the other side of the wound and finished taking the armor off.

Niallen was lowered back to the ground slowly, but yet another noise of discomfort came from his throat.

"Sorry, sorry." Asman muttered and ripped another piece from his tunic, gently pulling Niallen's own shirt up enough to see the wound.

The injury was leaking blood, and Asman inhaled sharply prior to pressing the cloth against it. Asman's eyes stung when Niallen let out a short yell, inhaling and exhaling quickly while his fist clenched around Asman's wrist.

"Shh, it's alright." Asman whispered and used his other hand to wipe the thin layer of sweat forming on Niallen's brow off, running his palm over the mans hair while he breathed through the pain.

Niallen's eyes shut and Asman continued to try and soothe him while he kept him palm pressing the cloth down into the wound.

Eventually, Niallen's breathing evened out while Asman sent little bursts of his magic into the wound. Niallen was not dying, but he could have, and that was all that mattered.

When he was sure that Niallen was either unconscious or sleeping, Asman sighed and laid his head on the mans arm.

They had won the battle, but had lost the lives of good men and women.

Chapter Nineteen:
Healing

The next day found Asman sitting on a cot parallel to Niallen.

The man was still unconscious, but at least his wound had been stitched up by Hutch. Asman's own deeper cuts getting the same treatment, but his were not as serious as some others.

Asman had not slept since the other night, but he could not even if he tried. He was worried that if he did so, Niallen would somehow get worse and die while he was not watching him.

Stulvon and Asman were the ones to carry him back to the fort, nearly tripping over the many dead soldiers laying in the clearing. Dahlia followed behind them with Niallen's armor and sword and Asman's own armor and black sword.

Each Guard had come in at least once to see how their leader was faring, and each time, Asman was still sitting next to him and watching to make sure he remained alive.

Hutch had said that it would not take long for Niallen to wake again, and Asman could see why as the man before him began to blink open his eyes.

"-sman?" Niallen muttered brokenly when he caught sight of said man.

Asman inhaled sharply and leaned forward, even though the cot he was sitting on only left enough room for his legs with how close it was to Niallen's.

"Yes. Yeah, I am here." Asman whispered back, hesitantly taking the mans hand in his; it should not have made his heart beat so fast, seeing as they had done it before.

"Is everyone alright?" Niallen asked quietly, fully awake and now looking around. The barrack was empty, since most of the Guard had gone to tend the wounded and care for the horses.

Asman frowned and exhaled shakily.

"Mostly. But... Hamen and Larrel." Asman squeezed lightly at Niallen's hand. "We gave them proper burials. Along with all the other soldiers that died."

Niallen shut his eyes and nodded, squeezing back at Asman's hand.

"What about the injured?" He asked and opened his eyes to look at Asman once more.

"Malon, Saraphina, and Strena were wounded, though they are recovering well. Everyone else has only minor cuts, Hutch and Elsten stitched us up."

"Hamen and Larrel, they had their swords?"

"Yes. I was- I was with Hamen, and Stulvon was with Larrel; they will be with the gods now." Asman absently rubbed his thumb against Niallen's knuckles. "Some of the soldiers were not as lucky, but I was told that the others fixed it."

"Good." Niallen sighed, his eyes moving to train on the ceiling of the barracks.

Asman remained silent and stared at Niallen unabashedly. He had been terrified when the he saw that sword go through Niallen's abdomen. Asman thought he had lost him.

Whether or not the man returned his feelings meant nothing if he was dead. Asman did not know if he could handle Niallen dying after all that had happened. Hamen and Larrel had died because they fought, and even though Asman knew they agreed to do so, it still sat unpleasantly in the back of his mind that none of this would have happened if he let Niallen do what he wanted to do in the first place.

There were fifty soldiers when they first came to the fort, and now there were only twenty. The Guard had lost two loved members and others were badly injured.

Asman had killed likely sixty men himself, more than half of them being those who wanted him to do so. The only thing he had ever killed before being with the Guard was a cow or two.

He had Death Magic that he could control, but what if later on it became harder? The voices had stopped only because he gave in to them; killing the soldiers quieted them, though Asman knew if he did not kill for a longer time they would start again.

The first sob that racked his body immediately caught Niallen's attention, even though Asman barely noticed.

His eyes clenched tight while the tears escaped unwillingly. Asman did not want to cry, he had done enough crying and it would do little to help his situation. He inhaled and exhaled greedily, trying to gather his emotions and stop crying.

"Asman..." Niallen spoke softly and squeezed his hand, only causing Asman to breath quicker. "Calm down, Asman. You are going to hurt yourself."

"Sorry. I am so sorry. I-I did not mean for anyone to get h-hurt. I thought, I thought I could- I thought killing them would make me feel better b-but it did not, and now people are dead because of me. I should have just left you alone when you got the letter, you would have made it so no one died but I f-fucked it all up." Asman sobbed heavily, his breath barely getting out with how much the emotions wrapped around his lungs. "I should have just wrote down my story and then drowned myself in a f-fucking river. Then no one would be dead and I would not have this magic that terrifies me all the time and you would not have to deal with me crying all the goddamn time and-"

"Asman, breath." Niallen interrupted quickly, shifting in the cot to better face Asman, but wincing at the pull in his wound.

Asman glanced up and sniffed harshly, eyes wide and shaking his head.

"Y-you should not move, your wound-"

"Is fine, Asman." Niallen interrupted again, continue to move until he was sitting up and pulling his legs into the same gap as Asman's.

Asman tried his best to wipe the tears from his face with one hand, and kept sniffing while Niallen placed one leg in between Asman's, boxing the latter in.

"Yes, people did die, and we will all miss them dearly, though do not think that it was your fault in any way. I could have denied your request and let you go on your own, but like I said before, you were right. Hamen and Larrel knew what they were getting themselves into the moment they signed their names as a Guard. Every one of us is hopeful that we could die the same as them, in battle, and on the winning side. Their families will be proud to know that they sacrificed their lives for Isadren and are with the gods." Niallen raised a hand and placed it on Asman's cheek, wiping away the tears still flowing. "I did not need you to come all the way to Isadren, Asman. I knew that I could have had you write a letter easily, everyone knew that. But I did not, because I also knew what kind of Guard you would be. I did not lie when I said you would be a good one.

"You rose to meet more than my expectations. You showed a strength that many before you did not have. Your magic takes far more than it gives, but you still used it to give those soldiers a better death. You used it to comfort me while I spoke of my family, and when I laid bleeding out in a field. Asman, you have more control over your magic than you think you do. When was the last time you got overwhelmed, or accidentally killed something you did not mean to? You know who your family is, and you know that you would never want to kill us. Because you love us and we love you, regardless of any magic or how many people you have killed."

Asman let out a shaky breath, staring back up at Niallen with helpless eyes while the man finished. He whimpered and kept Niallen's gaze, brown wet eyes looking into earnest and sincere blue.

Niallen shushed him and wrapped his free arm around Asman's shoulder, the latters face being brought into a bare neck. Asman tucked his own arm around Niallen's waist, not bothered that the man did not have a shirt on, but careful to avoid the linen wrapped around his wound.

"I was so scared." Asman whispered into the other mans skin. "I-I thought after that soldier stabbed you that you were going to die and... I was so scared, Niallen."

"I would never let something like a flesh wound kill me." Niallen huffed from behind him, his arm tightening slightly either way.

"I know. You have too much pride for that." Asman smiled softly, inhaling the scent of Niallen as well as he could with his stuffed nose.

Niallen chuckled and kept his arm around Asman, both of them just enjoying each other's embraces after such a long day and night.

Asman would have fallen asleep sitting there too, his eyes even closing and his breathing evening out before the door to the barracks opened.

"Asman. I brought you food and I swear to the gods if you do not eat I will personally shove it down your thr- Niallen!"

Dahlia had kicked open the door with two plates of food in hand before freezing and staring at the leader with wide eyes.

Her lips widened into a large smile while she skipped over to them and set the plates down on a table prior to jumping behind Niallen and hugging him.

Niallen grunted lightly at the movement but smiled nonetheless. Asman backed away slowly and grinned at Dahlia, his hand still holding Niallen's.

"Hello, Flower." Niallen said softly, a fond look on his face even though Dahlia could not see it.

"You are not supposed to scare us like that, you arse. I should go call the others in, they will want to see you." Dahlia squeezed Niallen's shoulders once more before backing away.

She was halfway to the door before she whipped back around and shot Asman a stern look.

"You need to eat too. It is not healthy to go so long without food, especially since you have not been sleeping either." Dahlia pointed a finger and Asman grimaced while nodding.

This seemed to appease the woman as she turned back around and walked out of the door.

"You have not slept or ate yet? Asman, you should not do that." Niallen frowned at the smaller man, who sighed.

"I know, do not worry Dahlia has already hounded me for it." Asman waved a hand and dropped Niallen's so that he could stand, walking over to where Dahlia had put the food down.

The plates had a simple meal of red meat, potatoes, and carrots on it that honestly made Asman realize just how hungry he was. He had not eaten since the day before last, as he was not especially hungry while looking at Niallen wounded on a cot.

He handed one plate to Niallen and sat back down, this time only next to the man and not practically on top of him.

They ate silently all until the door opened again and the Guard began flooding in. Niallen hurriedly took a few more bites before setting the plate down on the cot. Asman did so too once Niallen tried to start standing and winced.

"Careful." Asman muttered and stood in order to help the man rise from the cot. He easily shot out a leg to kick the cot he had been sitting on back and let Niallen use his shoulder and arm for leverage.

When the man was standing stably, Asman let go and sat back down to finish the food, not wanting Dahlia to force feed him the rest.

The Guard had filed in easily, only twenty-one compared to the twenty-three it had been previously. Niallen smiled through a wince as he held a hand to his side and walked into the group.

Asman watched from afar while Niallen gave and received hugs, some of the times grimacing but waving off any apologies from the others.

This continued till the sky outside was dark, and the cots had moved to the center cooking fire once more.

The Guard spoke of Hamen and Larrel, telling stories about them and drinking the little amount of ale that the fort had stocked away. Asman sat next to Niallen once more, obviously meaning that they were going to sleep next to each other also with how the rickety wooden beds were placed.

The last time they slept next to each other, Asman had not cared due to how the night had ended. Being woken up in the morning by an attack certainly did not help the situation either. But now, they were celebrating a victory and Asman was happy, so he focused more on the things that made him so. This included Niallen and how close they were.

The memory of the way the man had held him earlier made Asman's heart beat dangerously and a blush appear at his cheeks, though it could easily be blamed on the ale they had been drinking.

There was little doubt in Asman's mind that this was in any way romantic, they way that the man had acted, Asman was under the impression that was something you do with someone you did not have feelings for or had very many feelings for. Seeing as Asman was not exactly Niallen's best choice, he opted for the former.

Still, to see that man happy, with his family surrounding him and not much to worry about in the world. Asman would love to see that everyday, even if Niallen did not think of him in a romantic way.

He had gone through times like this when he was a teen, just then realizing he like men. There was a boy similar in age to him that Asman thought was gorgeous. He laid awake at nights thinking about that boy and him being romantic.

But... Niallen seemed different in a way. Niallen knew him, his past and his personality. Not only was he handsome, but he was a good man and a good leader. He saved Asman and trained him to be a good Guard, all because he trusted that Asman would be a good one.

Niallen loved his family, both in Isadren and the Guard; and even after the losses he had gone through, still remained strong enough to keep his head when threats of that happening again arose.

Asman adored all those aspects of Niallen. He wished he was half the man Niallen was, but he was not, and that seemed alright as long as the man was beside him.

He loved the caring nature of him, and the way he joked with the Guard although he was their leader. Asman loved the relationships and bonds formed because Niallen was just that good of a person. He loved the laugh Niallen made when Stulvon said something stupid, and how he called Dahlia Flower since he knew she liked it.

Asman loved everything about him, and even if he irritated him sometimes with his remarks, Asman... Asman loved him.

Asman loved Niallen.

Chapter Twenty:
Ice

The next morning was the day that the Guard set out fro the Isadren Capital.

Asman had finally gotten a good nights rest, even after realizing he was in love with Niallen and then proceeding to sleep next to the man. Nothing happened, and they remained on separate beds, but it was still closer than usual.

Either way, Asman woke with Niallen already saying his goodbyes to the Commander, who was recovering from her own wounds from the battle. Niallen's wound seemed to be nothing but an after thought to him, which aggravated Asman.

Just after sunrise, the Guard was already back on the road north; Cedran and the other horses seemed glad to be out of the fort and walking again.

Asman and Dahlia decided to walk up front due to Asman having to straining to see Niallen. Dahlia laughed and joked about it up until they were just behind the man. Asman could safely say that it was because he was worried Niallen's wound would cause him to fall off

Berry. There was also the fact of Asman just wanting to be near him, but he was also very worried.

Traveling to the Capital would only take a week, but Asman was fine with that. Every single village or town they came across had Asman in awe.

The foods, the people, even the smell, were far greater than any Feliasian town he had been to.

Not only were the towns amazing, but Asman could tell that there would be snow soon. The cold chill in the air enough to make Niallen buy him another cloak, though it seemed the man did not have to buy it at all.

The man that he had gotten it from knew who they were and had felt it was his honor to gift a new Guard a cloak. Asman could have cried he was so happy.

With a new fur lined and solid crimson cloak, Asman was even warmer and more willing to go and see all Isadren had to offer.

It was the fourth day of traveling in Isadren that they finally came across snow.

Thick flakes showered down from the clouds, dusting their cloak hoods and the horses manes. The trees gathered piles of the white fluff on their branches, and the grass became hidden beneath the sheets of it.

Asman could not stop looking around, his mouth wide and smiling while sending childish and excited looks everywhere. The Guard playfully mocked, saying his face would break if his smile got any wider. Asman only quipped for them to shut the fuck up and then continued to tip his head back, gathering the large flakes on his tongue.

When the snow became deep enough and the Guard had paused at a village for the night, Niallen and Dahlia took him out to a clearing to play in the snow.

Asman flopped face first into it as soon as he ran into the field, laughing and shaking away the clumps of melting snow. His leather armor made an imprint in the snow, and soon enough he was hauling both of the others down into the bank with him.

"You act as if it has never snowed in Felias." Dahlia teased while they sprawled out, arms and legs overlapping each other.

"Well, it has! But never like this! It would always melt before it could gather." Asman laughed out, gesturing wildly to the white forest around them. It was no longer snowing, but he was sure if he stood under a tree and tapped a branch he could make it happen again.

"Then we should be the ones to tell you that being outside while it is this cold for too long will get you sick." Niallen chuckled, sitting up and shaking the snow off his cloak.

"Oh, you are no fun. We can stay out here a bit longer." Dahlia smiled and waved a dismissive hand at Niallen, who had stood and was now working on patting the rest of the snow off, his back facing Asman.

"Fine, but when you two get-"

Asman giggled at the sight of Niallen, a splatter of snow where the former had thrown a ball of snow at his back.

He did not think the snow would stick together so well, but he was glad that it did. The look on Niallen's face when he turned being one of the best Asman had seen, causing him to break out in laughter against Dahlia.

Niallen grinned and leaned down, setting his own hands into the snow and gathering it into a sphere. Asman scrambled to make another ball, but was not fast enough as snow broke over his head and a yelp sounded from him.

Dahlia had taken her own time to start throwing snow at Niallen, who smiled and began his attack on both of them instead.

The snowball fight continued until Asman's fingers were red and sore from the bitter cold, and Niallen finally called a truce under the rapidly rising moon.

Asman went to sleep that night happier than he had ever been. With the fire blazing in his and Dahlias room and warming it against the frigid weather outside, Asman fell asleep with a smile still on his face.

Two days after that, Asman finally told Dahlia that he loved Niallen.

He had purposefully stuck to the back of the group, far enough that none of the Guards could hear what he had to say.

Asman told her quietly and with a heavy blush, but she only chuckled and nodded.

"Asman, we all can tell that there is something going on between you two." She started, her eyebrows raised beneath strands of brunette hair; most of those with long hair were keeping it down now with the cold. "Niallen has never gotten so close to someone that quick, especially not telling them about his family. There is also the very obvious way you look at him; like he hung the stars and moon."

Asman flushed deeper and huffed, staring back at Dahlia with a disbelieving look.

"We are friends. I might look at him like that, but... I do not think he treats me differently than any of the other Guards."

"Az, he did not even tell Stulvon about his family until they had known each other for three years. I do not know all of it and I have known him for five. It took you just over a fortnight to know everything." Dahlia scoffed a laugh, the sound and words causing Asman to frown.

"Good friends, then?"

"More than friends, Asman. Is it so crazy to you that he could actually return your feelings? You know he likes men too, and even he is allowed to find someone to love."

Asman glanced to Cedrans mane, trying not to show Dahlia what he was truly thinking. She had a habit of being able to tell things about him just by looking at his eyes.

"I-I know he is. I only want him to be happy, and I do not think I can give him that." Asman ignored the way his eyes and nose began prickling. "Niallen deserves to have someone stable and certain. I still do not know if my magic will flare up again and what will happen once we get to the Capital. He does not deserve to have to worry about that all the time; I think he has gotten enough of it in the past month."

Dahlia pulled her horse closer to Asman, placing a hand onto his legs and squeezing gently.

"Do you not think that is his choice to make?" She said quietly, her tone soft yet sharp at the same time. "As Niallen's friend, I will say safely that you both deserve each other. You could ask Stulvon, or any of the Guards the same thing and they will say that too. Both of you have gone through things, but both of you also help each other with them. The way you look at him and the way he looks at you... Az, do not throw away something that could be so good for you."

Asman sniffed away the tears forming and exhaled a shaky laugh, nodding at Dahlia after a short glance. His hood was partly over his face, so it obscured half the look.

"Thank you, Dahlia."

"Of course, Azzy."

———————————

Coming up to the Capital left Asman in more shock than seeing snow for the first time.

The outer city alone was larger than he had ever seen, he could compare it to perhaps ten Stelai's just around the Capital. There were whole streets lined with vendors, and large amounts of people walking around.

Many people paid their respects to the Guard by handing various foods or textiles to each member. Asman himself got a few loaves of bread and a thick woven tunic; the man who gave it to him saying he could tell that Asman was not used to the cold.

Although Asman felt bad for taking things from people he did not know, it seemed rude for him to deny any gifts sent his way.

The horses were pet and praised, as to the Isadrenians, they were just as important as the riders. Asman wholly agreed with this and made sure to tell those who complimented Cedran thank you.

The children in the streets sometimes worried Asman with how they would weave in and out between the horses and Guards, laughing and waving to them. Their parents seemed to try and keep them to the sidelines, but some still broke through anyway.

The closer they got to the Capitals castle, the more the streets were lined with finer houses and inns. At a specific house, the Guard stopped and watched while Nyana and Rhinn quickly dismounted.

The older woman and young child standing at the door rushing to meet them in familiar embraces. Asman smiled while Nyana kneeled to grasp at the young boy, hiding her sobs of happiness in his hair. Rhinn fondly talking to the woman and grinning widely.

After a heartfelt moment, Nyana and Rhinn both stated they would talk to the Guard later. Everyone obviously saying it was no issue and letting the couple reconnect with their son and Rhinn's mother.

A few others left after that, Marrion greeting her husband at their home, Hilcren returning to his parents along with Hutch to his own, Brandla jumping into her fathers arms as if she was not forty four and instead six.

Dahlia left with Cheden and Teran, the three of them having a house together. She stated that whenever Asman was finished talking with the Queen, he was welcome to come visit or even stay with them. Asman only nodded and gave her a hug; he did not know what would actually happen after him and the Queen spoke.

One by one, the Guard dissipated to their own houses or rooms at an Inn. This left only Asman, Niallen, Stulvon, and Saraphina, who's family apparently lived in the Castle.

Said Castle was the grandest building Asman could have ever hoped to have seen.

The walls were stone, the towers tall enough that Asman could hardly see where they ended. Each window glistened off the snow that sat in sheets across the sills and walkways. The main courtyard that the Guard first walked into was filled with trees, small sprinklings of snow glittering down with the wind.

Asman was in awe of it all.

Not only was the exterior of the Castle gorgeous, but the interior was dressed in elegance and beauty also.

Banners that held the Isadrenian sigil waved slowly on the walls, the dark blue and black popping against the grey of the stone bricks. The sigil was that of an owl, gripping a sword between its talons as it took flight in an endless sky. Asman found himself adoring it.

Added to the underlying sense of wonder, there was a greater sense of anxiety about what was to come.

Asman was sure the Queen would listen to him, but what would happen after? Him being Feliasian did not seem to matter all that much, though perhaps his magic did? Asman could be seen as dangerous easily with what his magic could do to some. Maybe the Queen would see him as a threat and execute him?

These thoughts flooded through his mind quickly, seemingly getting faster while the four remaining Guards entered the main hall. The entryway having various people standing around chatting, including two men that looked similar to Niallen.

"Niallen!" The shorter one called, a smile breaking his once somber look. The other male grinned shortly as Asman felt the connection click.

These two where Niallen's brothers. The shorter and younger one very clearly being Desmond and the older more serious one being Rossnan.

Niallen smiled and led the group over to them, immediately grabbing his brothers both into a wide hug. Though, he pulled away just to turn to Asman.

"Asman, I would like you to meet my Brothers, Desmond and Rossnan. Des, Ross, this is Asman, a new Guard this month." Niallen placed a hand on Asman's shoulder proudly, causing the one under it to blush slightly.

"It is nice to meet you, Asman." Rossnan smiled and bowed his head a little, Asman giving an embarrassed grin and doing the same.

"Nice to meet you too." Asman spoke quietly, but loud enough so that the other would hear.

"Wow, Niallen has never introduced such a new Guard member to us like this. Are you two fucking?" Desmond asked crudely and tilted his head like a dog.

Asmans face immediately erupted in flames, his mouth dropping down while his throat dried and failed to come up with words.

"Gods, Desmond, do you have to say shite like that? Leave the lad alone." Rossnan glared shortly at his brother, then turning his attention to the two smiling Guards off to the side. "Stulvon, Princess, it is great to finally meet you, Niallen has spoke highly of you both."

The other two greeted Rossnan back casually, leaving Asman to try and loose the blush on his face while avoiding eye contact with Niallen.

Niallen and the others allowed him to do so, Asman cursing himself for reacting so obviously at such a simple question. If Niallen did not know of his feelings now, that had been a sure hint in the right direction.

"Rossnan... why are you here?" Niallen asked after a moment, his voice having a certain fearful twinge to it.

"Ah. Yes, we should... we should speak, Niallen. Alone, if possible. I know you likely need to speak to the Queen-"

"No, no, I can talk to her later. It-It is about mother, is it not?" Niallen frowned and exhaled shakily, running a hand through his hair.

Rossnan and Desmond did not say anything, but the silence somehow spoke volumes.

"Stulvon, if you could take Asman to the throne room? I am sure the Queen already knows about..." Niallen glanced to the floor before inhaling sharply. "Asman, I am sorry I will not be there."

Asman shook his head and stared at the man with a frown.

"I will be fine. We will talk later, yes?"

Niallen nodded easily and sent a small yet sad smile to Asman. The latter sighed gently before pulling Niallen into a hug.

"It will be alright, Niallen." Asman whispered, only keeping the embrace lasting long enough for his message to get across before retreating.

Stulvon and Saraphina guided Asman away and back onto the path they had originally been taking.

Asman glanced back to Niallen once to see that his brothers were also guiding them away and into a separate room.

He sighed and focused back onto the larger door that they were approaching, two guards stationed outside that began opening the doors as soon as they spotted them.

This would be his first time speaking to royalty. Though, perhaps it would also be his last.

Chapter Twenty-One: Pride

"Saraphina, dear heart!"

Asman looked to where said Guard was walking swiftly up towards the Queen before both were wrapped in a hug.

"Grandmother, how are you?" Saraphina smiled, her voice partially blocked from it being facing a wall, but Asman was sure that was what he heard.

So when Rossnan called her princess it was not a joke. Saraphina was actually a princess. It did not shock Asman, per say, but it was something he had not even thought of before. Saraphina was very masculine and was not shy about her love for women; both her and Dahlia had also not been shy about the ongoing sex between them.

The two exchanged pleasantries while Asman focused his attention back to where he was, taking in the room and the ruler at its throne.

The ceilings were high, with large glass windows behind the ever large throne. The seat itself being a deep Isadren blue and dull silver steel. There was a rug laid out all the way up the stairs and beneath the claw footed legs of the throne, though it was black instead and thick beneath Asman's boots. He felt oddly bad standing on it and perhaps getting it dirty.

The royal woman standing in front of the throne was beautiful also.

The Queens gown was a deep red, with lace wrapping the bodice in the same color. Thick lined sleeves draped down to her wrists, that along with her neck, ears, and fingers, held gorgeous jewelry. The gems and stones within them catching on the candlelight within the room.

Her hair was grey, and her face wrinkled with age, but she still held an aura of the brilliantness reserved for being a Queen; that which was clear from the silver circlet crown placed gently on the short curls of her hair.

"You must be Asman. It is so nice to meet you after all these weeks. I am Queen Kelnua of Isadren."

Asman snapped his gaze up to finally meet the Queens, before realizing he was taking too long to answer and sputtering.

"I-It is nice to meet you too, your highness." Asman spoke as confidently as he could and bowed, his hands clasping behind his back.

"We have a lot to talk about do we not?" The Queen chuckled a bit, Asman noticing that Saraphina had begun walking over to a side room quickly. "Stulvon, as nice as it is to see you, your husband has been a pain in my arse ever since we heard the Guard was close. Go see him, would you?"

Stulvon snorted and nodded to the Queen before patting Asman on the back then walking back the same way as Saraphina. Asman had not known Stulvon had a husband, but then again, he knew little about the quiet man.

Asman glanced nervously around the room, finding only him, the Queen, and maybe four guards in the throne room.

"Asman, come sit, would you?" The Queen sighed as she sat down gently on one of the steps up to the throne, patting the place next to her easily.

He swallowed and nodded, rushing forward to follow her orders. His hands unclasped around his back and clasped again in his lap, his eyes focused on the black surface they sat on. Asman felt so on edge, unaware of what was considered disrespectful when speaking with a Queen.

"I imagine this must be very different than where you were just a month ago, yes?" Queen Kelnua smiled gently, her hands mirroring Asman's.

"Yes, ma'am." He whispered and nodded back.

"You can just call me Kelnua, if that makes this easier. I know the subjects we will be speaking of are rather personal." Queen Kelnua said with a sad smile, her gaze directed at Asman even if the latter was too scared to return it.

His heart was beating quickly, his palms cold and sweaty against each other. It was far different from the nervousness he felt around Niallen.

"I already know what happened to Thamor. Niallen wrote to me about it the moment they found you, and we do not need to speak of it, but I would prefer to hear your side of the story."

Asman inhaled deeply and steadied himself, glancing into the Queens light blue grey eyes for the first time.

"Me and my brother were just going to bed." Asman began, thinking back to all the times he had gone over what he would say to the Queen. "The first scream made him get up, but the soldiers were already breaking into the houses. If they could not break in, they set the house on fire. One of them came into our house and pinned my brother by the neck with his sword. I was close to the door, and the soldier was focused on him, so... so Sam told me to run. The soldier slit his throat and I ran."

Asman shut his eyes briefly and exhaled shakily; he had not told anyone what had all happened that night, not even Niallen.

"While I was running, a soldier caught on and began chasing me. He caught up once and gave me a wound, but I continued and ended up making it out into the forest. I was knocked unconscious from blood loss and then Niallen found me." Asman finished and opened his eyes once more to face Kelnua, her eyes full of sadness likely just as his.

He waited for her to speak, which took a moment as she thought through what he had said.

"I am sorry that happened to you, Asman. It was a pointless attack by Osetren that resulted in needless deaths." Kilnua reached out and took hold of Asman's hands with hers, enveloping his in a kind warmth.

"Do you know why he did it?" Asman asked quietly, calming slightly now that he had said his piece. There was still the bit about his magic left though.

"We believe it was an attempt to worsen Isadrens reputation." Kilnua explained with a sigh. "It is not the first time that Osetren has blamed an attack on us when he was the one who ordered it. More and more people are beginning to realize that Isadrenians are similar to their own selves. If Osetren were to loose the hatred, then men would not want to fight for him."

Asman nodded and stared back down to the carpet, anger swelling inside of his gut.

"Thamor was a pawn."

"To King Osetren, yes."

Asman frowned tightly. He was aware that King Osetren did not care about Thamor, but he would have never guessed that he would kill a whole village just to worsen the reputation of another kingdom.

"Asman, I would hate to keep you here all night, so perhaps we could talk about your magic?"

He stiffened at that, hating the way her voice dropped to a lower volume. Asman knew that this magic was bad, even where mostly everyone is accepted.

"There is not much to say. I have Death Magic that I did not know about till I signed my name as a Guard. I have been training to keep it under control but I could still be a threat if I loose it again." Asman's voice shook slightly while he attempted to maintain a neutral tone.

"Niallen has said that you have remarkable control over your magic, Asman." The Queen squeezed gently at his hands. "I am not worried about you becoming a threat. At least, not to Isadren. We have not lied to you, or hurt the ones you loved. I am sure Niallen has told you the real reason he wanted you to come here, and you yourself know the reason you wanted to be a prisoner for a short time.

"You fought for Isadren, Asman. You risked your life to defeat the Feliasians that had gotten across the border, and Isadren will forever be thankful for that. We take battle and honor very seriously here, and to fight for someone is to bond with them until you either die or fight for another."

"I am afraid it sometimes is too hard for me to control my magic at times. There are almost always the voices of The Dead whispering in the back of my mind. When I get overwhelmed, they become louder until I do what they wish. They are only calm now because of how many I killed at the border." Asman confessed; he felt as if he needed to prove himself a threat so that Kilnua would make sure her people were safe from him.

"We have many different Mages here that can help you with those voices. Many of those who have Moon or Sun Magic hear the voice of them in their mind also. I realize Teran is the only mage in the Guard beside you, but there are so many more in Isadren that can help you. Though, with how much Niallen praises your progress, I do not think you need it." Kilnua smiled softly and Asman blushed lightly.

"So, you are not going to kill me?" He asked softly, but not softly enough so that one of the guards standing nearby shifted unhappily.

"Gods no, my boy. There is absolutely no reason for you to die. Besides, do you know how upset Niallen would be? I am sure he would never forgive me and I love that kid, so that cannot happen." Kilnua let go of Asman's hands in order to wave a hand dismissively.

Asman let go a sigh of relief at last, his back hunching slightly and relaxing from where it had been straight up.

"Oh, Asman. You have a lot to learn about Isadren yet." Kilua chuckled quietly before dropping her smile a bit. "Speaking of Niallen. While he was gone, his mother passed away. I realize perhaps you do not return his feelings, but he could want someone nearby while he mourns."

Asman froze and stared at the Queen, looking for any hint of a jest or smile. He only found a slightly confused look and sadness.

"His feelings?" Asman whispered, still processing what she had said.

Niallen sent letters to the Queen all the time; practically every other night there was another one to write or read. Asman had only told Dahlia that he loved Niallen. The only way that the Queen could be messing with him is if Niallen somehow realized that Asman loved him and had the Queen of Isadren in on a demented joke. All which seemed something the man would not do.

"Asman, Niallen has said that you like men, but I also know how Felias can be when it comes to those sorts of relationships. If you do not return his feelings, I should hope you will not mock him or judge him." Kilnua had a stern look on her face that was too serious to be joking.

Dahlia was right. Niallen had feelings for him also.

Asman could not think even if he tried, there was only the singular thought of Niallen having feelings for him that continued to bounced around into every single part of his mind.

"Asman. If you do not love him back then you should tell him this, though perhaps not now. His mother was dear to him, and this death will hit him hard."

Oh, oh, now there were two thoughts. Niallen loved him back and Niallen's mother was dead.

"Your highness, I love him. I am in love with Niallen." Asman exhaled shakily with a small smile that quickly wiped from his face. "His mother... He said Rossnan and his family stayed with her in the mountains. How did she die?"

The Queen sighed softly and grimaced, standing up and sitting back down in her throne. Asman stayed seated at the steps.

"She became ill the spring after Niallen left. The healer said that she had likely the same illness as their father; it happens to many, and is unfortunately fatal."

Asman frowned and nodded. He understood all too well this sickness that stole loved ones in just a matter of one season.

"You truly love him?" She asked genuinely, a hand coming to splay across the arm of the throne.

"Yes. I- Dahlia had said he returned my feeelings after I told her a couple days ago that I loved him. I did not believe her." Asman huffed and thought back to the conversation.

"Do you believe me? Because Asman, this love that he has, it is not one you take lightly."

"I do. This- I have never loved someone like this before. Not so quickly, or deeply. I was ready for him to reject me, but I was also ready to stay with him, no matter if he loved me back or not." Asman looked to the floor with a blush; it was odd talking to a stranger about how much he was in love with his friend. Especially odder seeing as the stranger was the Queen of Isadren.

"Good, though you have no reason to think like that now. He deserves to have someone like you with him always. Like he needs you now." The Queen stood again and held out a hand for Asman. "I am sorry to keep you for so long, but I am glad we have had the chance to do so."

Asman took the offered hand and stood also, not actually using Kilnua at all. He only smiled softly and nodded.

"Now, I will have one of the guards take you to his room. I am sure his brothers have left by now. Please, make sure he is alright for me?"

"Of course, Your Highness."

Chapter Twenty-Two: Love

Asman stood silently outside of Niallen's room. The guard who had brought him having left a short moment ago.

He was slightly fearful of actually talking to Niallen now that he knew the truth of their feelings for each other. Asman had never spoken to the man while there was a clear possibility for them to be together.

But regardless of any romantic feelings, Niallen had just lost his mother and it would be terrible of Asman to try and focus on love when the other man was hurting.

"Niallen?" Asman finally called out and knocked on the wooden door. "I thought we could talk some. If you wanted, that is."

He waited and listened for any sign that the man was actually in the room, jumping when the door opened without any sound.

Ignoring the lack of noise, Asman just took in the sight of Niallen, frowning when he saw the mans state.

Niallen's hair was down and mussed up as if he had been lying on it. His armor was off, leaving him in just the undershirt and the pair of trousers he normally wore to sleep. The shirt was open near the top and exposing his chest, but Asman ignored it for favor of his eyes.

His eyes were dull, normally having a fire or happiness or anger at least, in them. Now, the blue eyes were sad and tired.

"Are you alright?" Asman questioned softly, knowing the answer anyway.

Niallen shook his head slightly, shutting his eyes for a moment before inhaling deeply and leaning over to allow Asman in.

The room was somehow so very Niallen; a bed, a desk, a wardrobe, a couple chests, a table, and the many different items pinned to the walls that obviously were gifts. Little hand sewn textiles, or the Isadrenian banner across the mantle place.

Once Niallen had shut the door behind him, Asman watched while he walked over to sit on the bed. The blankets and pillows moved to show that Niallen had in fact been lying down.

"Everything went okay with Queen Kilnua." Asman stated carefully and stood awkwardly in the middle of the room.

Niallen nodded and avoided eye contact, instead staring off to the wooden floor while deep in thought.

Asman went quiet for a moment, waiting for Niallen to start saying something, anything, about how he was feeling. When he got impatient though, he walked forward and sat next to the man on his bed.

"Niallen..."

"My mother is dead." He finally said, still staring at the floor. "She-She had the same illness father did and... and she's dead."

Niallen's voice was tight and thick, holding back too many emotions in favor of being strong.

"I know. Do you want to talk about what you are feeling at all?" Asman asked softly and watched Niallen face him with a desperate look; something that Asman had never seen on the man. "Do you... do you not know how to feel?"

Niallen shook his head again, his nose reddening along with his eyes. Asman frowned and reached out for Niallen's hand, the other automatically grasping for it.

"W-with my father and Rasina, we needed to stay strong for my mother. If we showed we were hurt by it then she would go too deep into her thoughts. So-So we did not cry and kept our backs straight... Asman, I do not know what to do." Niallen huffed out a glanced frantically from Asman's eyes to the floor.

Asman used his free hand to steady Niallen, holding his cheek in place and keeping blue eyes on brown.

"Niallen, do what you feel you need to do. Cry, scream, hit something, just let yourself react. You lost someone you were close to, and you do not need to be strong after that." Asman watched steadily as Niallen's composure cracked, a single tear sliding down his cheek.

The first sob to rake through Niallen sent a painful clench in Asman's heart, and when more came, it was enough to pull the man into a tight embrace.

Niallen responded by wrapping his arms around Asman's waist, the latter going around his shoulder and rubbing his hand smoothly up and down Niallen's back.

The tears from Niallen soaked into the collar of Asman's tunic, but he could not care less as he tried to soothe the crying man. When the hair tickling his face came too apparent, Asman switched to combing Niallen's hair back with his fingers and running his nails across his scalp.

Asman tried his best to whisper words of comfort, the only thing he did not say was 'I love you.' which Asman knew was not the moment for something like that.

Niallen cried for long time, sometimes sobbing and sometimes just breathing through it. He sniffled and held tightly onto Asman, the latter only holding him tighter also and inhaling deeply. Asman was withholding his own tears, hating having to see the man he loved in pain.

Once the tears slowed, Niallen finally pulled back gently. His hands came back from behind Asman in order to wipe quickly at his eyes and nose. There was an almost embarrassed look on his face that made Asman frown.

Asman began glancing around to try and find Niallen's water or something similar. Spotting a pitcher and cup on the table, Asman hesitantly stood and left the man for a moment in order to pour him a cup.

Niallen took the water from Asman when he held it out, the other watching while Niallen drank down its contents slowly. It was important to keep water in your body after crying for so long; Asman knew first hand how terrible it could make you feel.

"Do you feel better?" Asman whispered once he sat back down on the bed, cup forgotten on the nightstand.

Niallen nodded silently and shut his eyes, bringing a hand up to rub idly at his head.

"How about you lie down? I can blow out the candles and tend to the fire. The sun has set anyway, and it has been a long day- and year, for you." Asman hummed and stood, making enough room for Niallen to lay down across the bed.

While Niallen did as asked, Asman did as he said he would and went around the room, blowing the candles that had been lighting the room, out. The fire was almost dead, so Asman placed a few more logs on it before moving back to the bed.

Niallen was laid down, the blanket pulled up to his chin while the man stared off into nothing. Asman smiled softly and knelt down beside him.

"Would you prefer me to go so you can sleep?" Asman asked softly.

He would have liked to stay, but Asman could also respect if Niallen wanted him to leave for the night.

"Could you stay? If you wanted to go that is fine also." Niallen spoke quietly while Asman just shook his head lightly.

"I can stay until you fall asleep." Asman agreed just as softly; it felt wrong to be so loud at the moment.

"I do not think I can sleep now, Asman. Just come lie next to me? We can talk about what you and the Queen spoke of."

Asman flushed slightly and glanced to the ground.

"I have not changed or had a bath since before the battle, I do not think it is best if I get your bed dirty, Niallen."

It was true; the last bath he had was in a river just before the border, and seeing as it has been awhile since that river, Asman likely stank of dirt and old sweat. He hated it, but there were little chances they could find a lake or pond warm enough not to kill them in Isadren, and the Guard had been running low on coin for baths at the inns.

"To be honest, I have not either, so it is not as if my bed is clean as of now." Niallen grinned with a shrug and Asman sighed through his nose, giving in to the mans request.

It was getting to be amusing what revelations he had right before sharing a bed with Niallen. Whether it be realizing he loved Niallen, or Niallen loved him, they were always before sleeping with hum.

Before slipping under the blankets atop of the bed, Asman made sure to slip off his boots. Knowing that Niallen, who loved him back, was behind him lying on the other side of a real bed, waiting for Asman to join him in it was somehow more surreal than having magic.

The darkness of the room thankfully hid most of his blush, any hints of pinkness evident were disguised in the orange firelight.

Niallen had shifted onto his back once Asman laid, he was facing Niallen and on his side. Cots were far different then actual four poster wooden beds with a mattress and two pillows underneath each head.

"What did you and the Queen speak about?" Niallen finally asked after both men were settled.

"My version of what happened to my village, and a little about my magic." Asman replied, trying to at least lay his hand under his head so that not so much of his dirty face was touching the pillow. Though, it would be surprising to see since the fabric was dyed red.

"Did she say what would happen now?"

Asman avoided Niallen's eyes, instead staring at the soft eggshell colored sheets. The blankets matched the pillows as a deep red, and Asman found it funny since Niallen was leader of the Blood Guard and the color was almost blood like.

"No. She only told me that King Osetren used Thamor as a pawn in order to tip the scales in Felias' favor again, and that there were many different Mages who can help if my magic gets harder to control while I am here." Asman scratched idly at a fuzz on the sheets.

"You have not spoke about what happened that day much." Niallen stated, but Asman could tell it was a question for him to answer.

"There was not much to tell. I told you the important information and that was all I really felt as if talking about. I was mourning, still am, and I needed time to process I suppose." Asman shrugged and was lucky that thinking back to that day did not hurt as much.

He had survived the journey to Isadren, and had told his story to the Queen. This, being in the castle and safe from Felias, was all he ever stayed alive for. The chance to see Felias taken apart was also what would keep him wanting to stay alive; along with Niallen and the Guard, because they were his family now.

"At least it is over with. Though, now there is only the choice of what you will do." Niallen whispered the last part, his eyes staring up to the stone bricked ceiling.

"Niallen, I could never leave the Guard." Asman sighed gently, finally looking to the man. "They are my family, just as they are yours and we are theirs. Traveling was not so bad, and I would gladly help in trying to dismantle Felias."

Niallen looked over to Asman but did not say anything, an unidentifiable look crossing his face.

"I do not know if your offer still stands for me to continue being a Guard, but I will take whatever you give me." Asman's face prickled lightly with heat.

He still did not know if this was the time to talk about their feelings for each other. Though, Asman did not know how long he could keep from saying what he had been holding back for a week now.

Would it seem insensitive for him to talk about love and new beginnings right after the man had found out his mother died? Or would it brighten Niallen's mood maybe and make him feel better after such horrid news?

"You will always be welcome as a Guard, Asman." Niallen smiled softly down to the other man. "I was wary if you would want to stay now that you are actually here. You could find a practice in the city, or even travel further inland and settle down in a village."

Asman shook his head quickly; he could never live in a brand new city or village alone. Or without Niallen.

"I... I do not want to live somewhere, a village or city or castle, without you there with me, Niallen."

The room echoed the words, both men silent at what was clearly a confession of sort. Asman was frozen while he waited for a response, scared even though he knew Niallen's feelings for him.

Niallen's mouth parted slightly with shock, his eyes widened a tad as he stared down at Asman, the latter looking away with a blush. Gods, the man was still beautiful with a reddened nose and eyes.

"So-Sorry, that was... I should not have said that. You likely do not want to talk about that now, I am sorry. I should go." Asman stammered and ripped the blanket off of him, embarrassment flooding his body.

That was stupid. There were many reasons why Now would not have been a good time to basically tell Niallen he wanted to live with him.

"Asman. Asman, wait." Niallen called softly just as said man lifted off the bed and grabbed for his boots.

Before Asman could walk off, Niallen got up to kneel on the bed and grasp for Asman's wrist, holding tight to keep him there.

"Asman, just wait, alright? I am fine with talking about this now, so please do not run away from me." Niallen's voice sounded pleading, and it was the only thing that actually made Asman calm a bit and turn around.

"But, Niallen, y-your mother... I just, I should have waited to say something." Asman sighed sadly and shook his head.

Niallen stabilized himself on the bed, his knees still digging into the mattress while he gently pulled Asman back onto the bed.

"No, no, I am glad you did." Niallen smiled softly through a grimace, exhaling slowly when Asman sat back down against the backboard of the bed after setting his boots back down.

Niallen settled back down next to Asman, though he kept his hand on the latters wrist for a moment before sliding it down to intertwine with Asman's fingers.

Asman looked off into the blanket sprawled across the bed, mussed from where both of them had thrown it off in haste.

The silence remained thick in the air. Asman had no clue what he was meant to say to Niallen. Neither of them made a move to start the conversation they knew was coming.

The only sound in the room was that of the fireplace crackling and the distant city below the walls. Every rustle of movement made by him or Niallen was volumes louder than it should have been.

"Niallen, I-"

"I love you, Asman."

Asman's breath hitched and he finally shot a glance at Niallen, finding the mans face tinged a pleasant pink and his eyes trained on Asman.

"I-I love you too." Asman whispered, his eyes a little wide but a small smile finding its way onto his face also.

Niallen grinned widely and chuckled lowly, squeezing at Asman's hand. The man paused for a moment before making a noise in his throat.

"You mean- romantically? Right? Because I hop-"

"Yes, Niallen. Romantically." Asman smiled and rolled his eyes.

Niallen smiled and nodded, his giddy expression making Asman giggle. The former noticed this and smoothly pulled Asman's hand up to his lips, kissing at each knuckle in between his own.

Asman blushed and let him do so, feeling his heartbeat right beneath his skin. With a chuckle, he covered his face with his hand, knowing that Niallen could likely see the flush.

When the hand on his face was pulled away, Asman whined and cracked open his eyes to look at Niallen. The smile was still on his face even if he was embarrassed. Niallen kissed that hand too before sliding down to lie flat on the bed.

Asman followed after a persistent squeeze of his hand, very quickly realizing that Niallen was far closer this time while he pulled the blanket back over them.

Niallen's face was a short distance away, close enough that Asman could feel his breath puffing against his own lips. It would be so easy to just press forward...

Before Asman could have connected their lips, Niallen did so first. The warmness slightly shocked Asman and made him hum tightly.

Asman let go of Niallen's hand just so that he could place both of his against the mans cheeks, very ready to pull him back if need be. He had wanted to kiss Niallen for so long now, Asman would have to be dead in order to stop.

With Asman's hands on his face and neck, Niallen moved to wrap an arm around the others waist, pulling Asman in closer.

The feeling of Niallen's lips on his was unlike any others he had before. The merchant and bards, Wentt. All of them were nothing compared to having the man he loved slip a soft tongue across his own. Asman could not contain most of the noises he was making; hums and sighs that escaped each time they parted for a breath.

When they finally stopped kissing, both pairs of lips were red and swollen, spread thinner from the smiles they housed.

Asman yawned and cuddled into Niallen's chest, the hair exposed from his tunic tickling Asman's cheek and not bothering him in the least. Niallen pressed his own face into Asman's hair and wrapped both arms around the latter in different spots.

Both men warm and content for the night, it was easy and quick when they both drifted off.

Chapter Twenty-Three: Epilogue

The morning after that found Asman and Niallen still holding each other. The warm rays of morning light shining across Niallen's bed even if the room was chilled.

The fire had gone out over the course of the night, causing Asman to be woken by his toes chilled and his face attempting to bury itself deeper into Niallen's chest till he could not breath.

After many attempts to fall back asleep, Asman finally gave up and wiggled himself from the other mans hold, shivering while reigniting and stoking the fire. It felt nice to not have to worry about being back on the road as soon as he woke.

Instead, he could stand by the fire and warm himself while he waited for Niallen to wake. Which did not seem to take long seeing as the heat keeping him warm was gone.

Niallen slowly padded over to Asman, his bare feet slapping against hardwood that would have made Asman shriek if he did not have socks on. Niallen ignored what was likely ice cold floors to instead wrap his arms around Asman's shoulders with a hum.

While the fire crackled and the room filled with heat again, Asman kissed his love with a small smile fit only for quiet mornings.

That same day also contained a bath between them and a dinner with the Guard. The bath was full of scented oils and perhaps heavier kissing, but resulted in them both clean anyway.

The dinner was held at the castle and was stock full of food that the people of the Guard had not eaten in a year; some of the foods Asman had never eaten before in his life.

Niallen and Asman told the Guard that they were together now, and that Asman would be remaining in the Guard until further notice. The night ended in a very loud group of drunks, filling the castle with laughter and song.

Asman, for the next year, began learning more about his magic from the head Mage in the castle, the woman being personally appointed by the Queen. She taught him about what Death Magic truly could do and how to keep the voices calling for him to kill to a minimum.

There had not been a campaign for a long time. So, Niallen spent his days helping around the castle with chores, or having a seat in the war cabinet as an esteemed member. Desmond was less suited for battle plans and instead graduated to a spot on the civil disputes cabinet.

Rossnan and his family of four moved into the city nicely, his wife having knowledge of herbs led them to having an apothecary while her husband tried to learn to help.

The rest of the Guard did what they wanted. Some worked at temporary practices, and some joined the Royal Guard as intermittent soldiers for everyday guarding of the castle.

Each day, when the city and castle woke, Niallen and Asman were ready for the news that Felias was attacking the border again. With how the war was coming to a point, it was inevitable that one of those days would land them in the final battle.

Two winters after they had arrived, the news finally came.

With summer approaching quickly, the Feliasian armies had marched to the border. Thankfully, a letter from Fort Aidell stated that the armies would wait until Isadren had gathered their own fleet worth battling.

The letter included, by name, for the Blood Guard to be there. Calling especially for Niallen and the 'Vanien's Spawn'. Asman would have felt upset, but he had began worshipping the Isadrenian gods two springs ago.

At this new word, Queen Kelnua agreed to send a portion of their army; the others would lie back and wait if those at the border all perished.

Now, it is time to finally fight for the peace in Calia.

It was time, for the Fall of Felias.